YOUR ROAD.

YOUR CHOICES.

Adversity

Development

Character

Ownership

Leadership

Habits

AMANDA JO ERVEN, CPA, CIA, CFE

FOUR ACES PRESS

DENVER, CO

"Don't wait!!"

YOUR ROAD. YOUR CHOICES.
Copyright ©2021 by Amanda Jo Erven

Four Aces Press
Denver, CO

YOUR ROAD. YOUR CHOICES. /Amanda Jo Erven
Revised Edition
Original title: Our Choices on the Road of Life

ISBN 978-1-7337843-6-8

THIS BOOK DEDICATED TO MY HUSBAND:

For choosing to walk this road with me.

"Good things come to those who wait... but don't.
You deserve better than good."
– Amanda Jo Erven

YOUR ROAD. YOUR CHOICES.
CONTENTS

INTRODUCTION:

MY CHOICES. MY ROAD.

> *"One day I decided I was going to choose me.*
> *I haven't looked back since."*
> – Unknown

WALK FORWARD ONLY

MY ROAD HASN'T always been well paved and perfectly straight. Personally, I have often struggled to figure out who I am, what I should do, or where I should be. But what I have realized through each struggle *(yes, this is why we will discuss adversity first),* is that I made clear and distinct choices that set me on my current path. I did not leave my life up to chance, fate, or *"what may be."* I took charge of what I could, and walked forward, no matter what the road looked like... potholes, curves, sharp turns, hills... mountains... dirt, potholes.

Did I mention potholes?

A few years ago, I read the *"Autobiography in Five Short Chapters"* by Portia Nelson and it changed my life.

CHAPTER I

I walk down the street.
There is a deep hole in the sidewalk.
I fall in.
I am lost... I am helpless.
It isn't my fault.
It takes forever to find a way out.

CHAPTER II

I walk down the same street.
There is a deep hole in the sidewalk.
I pretend I don't see it.
I fall in again.
I can't believe I am in the same place.
But, it isn't my fault.
It still takes a long time to get out.

CHAPTER III

I walk down the same street.

There is a deep hole in the sidewalk.

I see it is there.

I still fall in... it's a habit... but,

my eyes are open.

I know where I am.

It is my fault.

I get out immediately.

CHAPTER IV

I walk down the same street.

There is a deep hole in the sidewalk.

I walk around it.

CHAPTER V

I walk down another street.

So, I ask you, what chapter are you on?

Today, I am happily on Chapter V. And this book is meant to show you how to be on Chapter V as well. Whether it resonates with you *professionally*, regarding your entire job, a project, a skill, or a goal that needs revisited... or whether it resonates with you *personally*, regarding a relationship, an environment, or a circumstance you need to change. At times, everyone is in need of a change.

Everyone is in need of a new street.

CHOICE VS. FATE

Four years ago, I found myself staring at a piece of paper that said I had a 45% chance of ovarian cancer and an 86% chance of breast cancer in my lifetime. And for a brief moment, I thought that was my fate. It, sadly, was the fate of my Grandmother and my only Aunt on my Father's side of the family, who both passed away at a very young age.

But quickly I determined that I had two choices on my road. To wallow in the *"what may be"* or to take proactive steps to change my so-called fate. I chose the latter. A full hysterectomy and a double mastectomy later, the piece of paper that said...

RESULT: POSITIVE
CLINICALLY SIGNIFICANT MUTATION IDENTIFIED
GENE: BRAC1 MUTATION
INTERPRETATION: HIGH CANCER RISK

...was put away in the drawer, where it still remains today.

Now, honestly, this was one of the easiest choices I have ever made. And *almost* everyone I have encountered agrees with the choice I made. So, I start with this one to just *"break the ice"* for you when it comes to choices.

Some are easy choices. Some are hard. Some choices, people immediately agree with. Some choices, people look at you differently. But no matter the situation, make the choice that propels you forward, down the right street for *YOU*. Don't leave your life up to fate.

HOW TO WALK DOWN ANOTHER STREET

We *all* make choices on this road called life. We make choices in our personal lives. We make choices in our professional lives. We make choices when encountering adversity. We make choices that reflect our character. We make choices that echo our feelings, attitude, motivation, and perspective. We make choices that form our identity and habits, both good and bad.

We make choices that shape our careers. We make choices about how we lead. We make choices that turn out to be mistakes. We make choices that turn out to be perfect, life-altering decisions.

We are the sum of our choices.
The choices you make, from this day forward, will determine your future.

Think for a moment about the reasons you may not be reaching your full potential. Really assess your personal and career accomplishments. What are you happy about? What is making you miserable *(at home or at work)?* What could *(should)* you change?

We are about to break down your current choices and turn them to actionable plans *(perhaps new choices completely)* for your *future* street. Each section of the book contains background material for what I believe to be the key life choices around *adversity, development, character, ownership, leadership, and habits.* The questions at the end of each section provide a framework for self-reflection, starting with an assessment of how your past and current choices are influencing your life.

ADVERSITY AND CHALLENGE

We have all heard that if adversity doesn't kill you, it will make you stronger. I'm pretty sure truer words have never been spoken. So, how do you handle the inevitable adversity in your life? Do you muddle through and come out feeling defeated and discouraged? Or, do you look back and believe that you are stronger and more confident because of the way you managed the challenge? What are your current *"adversity choices"* and are they serving you well? What should you change?

You can choose to embrace and manage adversity in a way that helps you surpass (not just meet) your life goals.

DEVELOPMENT AND EFFECTIVENESS

Do you like the image of yourself when you look in the mirror? *(Dig deeper than just the superficial.)* Does your level of knowledge and skills truly match the vision of you? Have you logically prepared yourself to accomplish all your ambitions? Do you have development plans? Is the plan reasonable and doable? Are you on track? Are you prepared to make the commitment of time and other resources? What are your current *"self-development"* choices and are they serving you well? What should you change?

You can choose to make self-development a priority and, in turn, change the trajectory of your life.

CHARACTER AND ETHICS

How is your moral compass? What is it built on? Do you know a moral or ethical dilemma when you see one? Does your compass match the environment that you are in? Does it match your associates and leaders at your organization? Does it match your friends and family? How do you react to moral dilemmas? What are your current *"character choices"* and are they serving you well? What should you change?

You can choose to uphold impeccable character, to be an everyday ethicist.

OWNERSHIP AND ENTREPRENEURSHIP

Regardless of your employment status – job/no job, self-employed/working for *"the man,"* big company/small company, public sector/private sector, for profit/nonprofit – we all have a perspective of what we do. Is it all about what we can do for ourselves? Or, is it all about what we can do for others *(life's customers)?* I call this the *"entrepreneurial"* part of you. How do you act and make life decisions? What are your current *"ownership choices"* and are they serving you well? What should you change?

> *You can choose to have an entrepreneurial spirit; you don't have to be an entrepreneur to think and act like one.*

Genuine Leadership

We are all leaders one way or another, formally in an organization hierarchy or informally amongst co-workers, mentees, or friends. So, how good of a leader are you? Have you established a genuine, effective leadership philosophy and do others willingly follow? Will your leadership qualities enable you to accomplish more *(or less)* in your life and career? What are your current *"leadership choices"* and are they serving you well? What should you change?

> *You can choose to lead others in a way that will change their life, and yours.*

Identity and Habits

Our habits reflect us for better or worse. Are your deep-rooted habits getting in the way of living your values and accomplishing your goals or are they the source of your success? Have you conducted an honest self-assessment and determined your identity? Do your habits support your optimum identity and do you minimize the unproductive habits and cultivate the productive ones? What are your current *"habit choices"* and are they serving you well? What should you change?

You can choose to build a life on good, productive habits and ditch the bad ones getting in your way.

THESE ARE OUR LIFE CHOICES.

"Each person's destiny is not a matter of chance; it's a matter of choice."
– S. Truett Cathy

YOUR ROAD. YOUR CHOICES.

Personal and professional growth can be haphazard *(learn the hard way)* or it can be the result of periodic self-assessment and a more productive planning and execution process.

A deliberate, *"choice-based," (remember the title of the book)* growth process starts with a self-assessment of where you are today. For example, what has been accomplished in your personal and professional life to date? Role models and mentors are no substitute for your own hard work and effort, but who and how have others *(relationships)* impacted your life?

Most believe that the greatest learning *(for better or worse)* occurs under adverse situations and how we handle adversity has a great impact on our long term success. So, what adversities have occurred in your life and how did they impact you?

Life is about building on strengths and learning from and overcoming weaknesses. So, what is your assessment *(also using honest feedback you have received from others)* of your greatest strengths? What are the areas that you would benefit from change and improvement?

The following questions are to get you thinking about your personal and professional road to date. This will lay the groundwork *(or dirt)* for identifying where change needs to occur... where different choices need to be made... where your road needs to be repaved.

This is the beginning of the rest of your life.

EXPLORE YOUR CHOICES FROM THE PAST.

What are your greatest personal accomplishments to date?

Who has had the biggest impact on your personal life? Was it positive or negative?

What are your greatest professional accomplishments to date?

Who has had the biggest impact on your professional life? Was it positive or negative?

What personal adversity or challenge have you faced?

What professional adversity or challenge have you faced?

How does adversity impact your life (e.g., physically, emotionally)?

What are your strengths that you build on?

What are your weaknesses that must be overcome?

What are your key character traits?

What are your core values?

How would you describe your entrepreneurial characteristics?

How would you describe your leadership characteristics?

What are your not-so-good habits?

What is your passion?

CHOOSING TO EMBRACE ADVERSITY:

THE ART OF THE STRUGGLE

"The most beautiful people I've known are those who have known trials,
have known struggles,
have known loss,
and have found their way out of the depths."
– Elizabeth Kübler-Ross

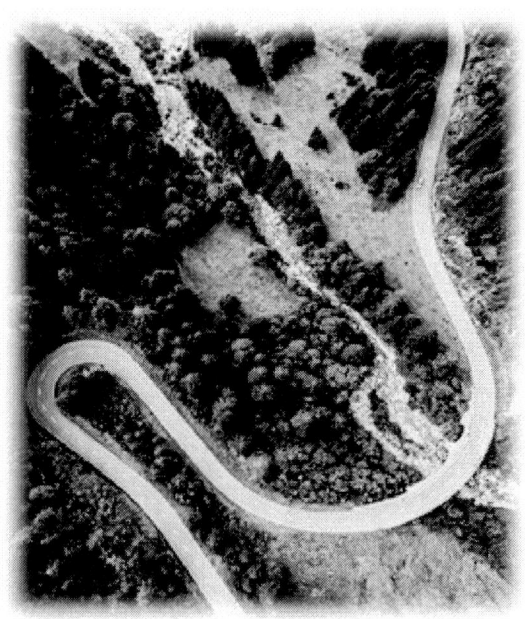

LIFE'S CURVES

WHEN WE LOOK BACK ON our lives and focus on times of adversity, we usually have a couple of immediate thoughts. One is that the period was very difficult and challenging and often mentality and emotionally painful. The second thought, at least after some time has passed and the mind is clear of the pain, is that we learned a lot.

We typically learn to avoid the circumstances that caused the adversity in the first place *(if within our control),* or learn how to better handle the specific adversity. We know we have been tested regarding how much we can take. Our strengths and weaknesses are magnified. We are out of balance from our normal, comfortable routine. We learn what we cannot do and, fortunately, we learn we *can* do things that we never imagined that we could do.

Suffering the loss of a loved one, experiencing a failed relationship, facing a significant health issue, losing a job that you loved *(or not)* all come to mind when we think about adversity and extraordinary challenges. A few people come to mind as well:

Itzhak Perlman

Born August 31, 1945

Internationally acclaimed violinist, conductor, and music teacher

Over the course of his career, Perlman has performed throughout the United States and worldwide. Perlman became interested in the violin as a small child but was denied admission to a conservatory because he was too small. He contracted polio at age four and has walked using leg braces and crutches since then, playing the violin only while seated.

Among numerous other awards over his lifetime, including Emmy and Grammy Awards, in 2015, he was awarded the Presidential Medal of Freedom: The highest civilian medal given to people who have made *"an especially meritorious contribution to the security or national interests of the United States, world peace, cultural or other significant public or private endeavors."*

Then there is...

Stephen Hawking

January 8, 1942 – March 14, 2018

World acclaimed theoretical physicist, writer, professor

Hawking was an English theoretical physicist, cosmologist, and author who was director of research for cosmology and a professor at the University of Cambridge. In 1963 (age 21), Hawking was diagnosed with an early-onset, slow-progressing form of amyotrophic lateral sclerosis (ALS), or Lou Gehrig's disease, that gradually paralyzed him. Even after the loss of his speech, he was still able to communicate through a speech-generating device, initially through use of a hand-held switch, and eventually by using a single cheek muscle. Through it all, he redefined our view of the universe.

****

The key is to embrace the adverse situation we have been placed in and use it to our advantage. Turn a negative into a positive. Use the events as an opportunity to grow personally and professionally. As author Bill George *(Find Your True North)* notes:

> *"Life is chock-full of potentially rich developmental experiences.*
> *Our challenge... is to identify those times that seem most interesting and squeeze them for all their worth."*

The first step when you see dark clouds ahead is embracing the commonly heard *(and not so commonly adopted)* mindset of the *"glass half full."* The other half of the glass is the discovery, learning, and growing you are about to experience. If you adopt a *"glass half empty"* approach, the discovery, learning, and growing will be delayed at best, and at worst, may never occur.

MY ADVERSITY ROAD: MY CHOICES

Like most of us, I have managed to rack up a few adverse and challenging periods in my life. Admittedly, some were self-induced, while others were pretty much out of my control. It really makes no difference – they all represented reality at the time. In the Introductory Chapter of this book, I began by sharing one of the adverse events that was very meaningful to me.

I asked you to do the same in the first exercise. Awareness and recognition is how we ultimately gain from our experiences.

To build on my adversity road, I want to share a second period of challenge I faced as a result of my proactive health story.

What I didn't realize was happening *(while I was busy making choices for myself and my health),* was that there was a huge impact on my career. Although I worked hard to not let the emotional and physical impacts of my surgeries *(6 surgeries within 22 months)* interfere with my work, the perception *(some real and some perceived)* was that it had. And it was brought to my attention rather abruptly.

As a result, I felt I had to make a choice of whether to continue my employment in a potentially toxic environment or make a job change. I had been at my employer for ten years and progressed nicely from a Senior Auditor to Internal Audit Director. I was professionally secure. I could continue in my current position and attempt to manage the situation. But I wasn't sure it was possible. There were also other things that did not sit well when it came to my professional environment; in fact, some we will touch on in other chapters in this book *(see the Choosing Impeccable Character chapter).*

My point? An adverse situation created by what I considered a significant health issue turned into another adverse event that was going to potentially change my professional career and my life. It was time, again, to make a choice.

Since my life's motto starts *"Good things come to those who wait... but don't,"* I didn't wait long at all. I quit my job. I decided to quickly fill up the other half of my glass, not focusing on the half that had evaporated in the blink of an eye. I founded my own professional services firm focusing on auditing, consulting, training, and education. I *"filled the glass"* with new experiences and new career challenges.

I rapidly acquired a new set of skills associated with my new *"glass"* – some seemingly obvious, like sales and marketing of my products and services, pricing and business negotiations, legal aspects of a small business, and small business accounting *(e.g., taxes – yikes, remember I'm an auditor).*

Then there was the web design and social media support, writing and book publication *(this is book #2),* higher education instruction *(I taught several college level courses for the first time),* professional firm certification accreditation *(with the National Association of State Boards of Accountancy),* and of course, the overall development of impactful and unique training material, for live and virtual settings *(learning how to succeed at webinars and podcasts could be a whole other book).*

And did I mention standing up in front of thousands of new people each month and projecting the confidence that you are meant to be there and that they should listen to you?

The learning never stops. And the list goes on of new challenges and experiences RISING FROM ADVERSITY. So you have to embrace the struggle. *Embrace your list.*

HOW DO YOU EMBRACE ADVERSITY?

First and foremost, use the adversity to gain a deeper meaning of life and understand that there are many things that occur in our lives that cannot be anticipated or controlled. It is not *(always)* your fault. **This is the acceptance stage.**

Reach out for support of family, friends *(likely some new and evolving friends),* professional contacts *(past and newly sought),* trusted advisors, and counselors. Seek professional counseling resources if you believe necessary and appropriate. *My therapist is my biggest fan.* **This is the advocacy stage.**

Conduct *(with or without professional help)* an internal self-assessment. Come to grips with your shortcomings and become more self-aware. Assess to what degree your own conduct contributed to the adversity *(but don't dwell on it).* Learn the lessons of the adversity and failings. To the degree that your actions are interrelated to the unintended adverse consequences, develop a plan to modify your behavior, skills, attitude, etc. **This is the assessment stage.**

After having conducted the internal assessment and implemented the changes, make a fresh start on your terms for the rest of your life. Learn to escape the adversity of the past by committing yourself to the present and the future. Move on. **This is the action stage.**

On the *"move on"* note, make the conscious decision to never look backwards *(remember the Introduction chapter "walk forward only"),* which often leads to reliving anger and resentment and blaming others. Looking backward at adversity can, in its most severe form, result in post-traumatic stress disorder (PTSD).

PTSD sufferers sometimes are unable to address or even acknowledge the underlying issues. Instead, believe that adverse traumatic experiences can result in post-traumatic growth (PTG). PTG starts with a self-awareness of life's uncertainties and taking personal responsibility to make necessary changes to change the events in the future. Nick Craig, the founder of the Authentic Leadership Institute, describes the PTG path for those experiencing adversity as moving from *"victims"* to *"survivors"* to *"thrivers."* *Be a thriver.*

Consider re-focusing at least part of your efforts externally to helping others who are facing similar adversities to those that you experienced. Personally, I have done this through my volunteer involvement with Susan G. Komen, whose mission is to invest in breakthrough research to prevent and cure breast cancer. Since my story began with prevention, it is fitting to continue supporting others on the road to prevention. I am the prototype for re-directing your energy. It has worked for me *(in many ways, this is just one example)*. Reframe your adversity to a newfound mission to address similar issues and to serve others.

Finally *(and similarly)*, put all your energy on the door that is opening, not on the door that is closing. Focus on the glass half full, not on the glass half empty. Adopt a *"growth mindset" (that is the new hip term, right?)*, invite change, continuously learn and adapt, and believe in self-development *(see the next chapter)*. The goal is to *"wake up smarter every day,"* according to author Steven Snyder.

See Exhibit I in the Appendix for a summarized *Embracing Adversity Growth Plan (EAGP)*.

Life's road is not always fair and predictable. It is imperfect and unpredictable. It has twists, turns, and curves. Adversity cannot be avoided. The important thing is how we use adversity and the challenges it presents to personally and professionally grow. If that is your outlook, if you embrace adversity, you will inevitably draw strength from your experiences and perhaps provide strength for others. *That is the real art of the struggle.*

Use adversity as an inspiration to gain new skills, develop a new attitude, and build new relationships. Use adversity as a reason to seek out support. Use adversity to re-set your goals.

Use adversity as a motivator for change. And, once again, don't... look... back.

THIS IS THE ADVERSITY CHOICE.

"Some people see a wall and assume that's the end of the journey. Others see it and decide it's just the beginning."
– Angelina Trevena

MY FAVORITE ADVERSITY QUOTES

"We are all faced with a series of great opportunities brilliantly disguised as impossible situations."
– Chuck Swindoll

"The obstacle in the path becomes the path... Within every obstacle is an opportunity to improve our condition."
– Ancient Zen Parable

"Bad companies are destroyed by crisis. Good companies survive them. Great companies are improved by them."
(Substitute *"people"* for companies)
– Andy Grove, former Intel CEO

"He who doesn't want to face challenges shall always face challenge."
– Ernest Agyemang Yeboah

"A challenge only becomes an obstacle when you bow to it."
– Ray Davis

"There is no education like adversity."
– Benjamin Disraeli

"We don't develop courage by being happy every day. We develop it by surviving difficult times and challenging adversity."
– Barbara De Angelis

"It's fine to celebrate success but it is more important to heed the lessons of failure."
– Bill Gates

EXPLORE YOUR ADVERSITY CHOICES.

What is the greatest personal adversity(s) that you have faced in your life?

What is the greatest professional adversity(s) that you have faced in your life?

<u>For each:</u>

What was your mindset/attitude at the time of the adversity?

What resources did you have to deal with the adversity?

How was the adversity resolved?

What changes were made?

What impact did the adversity have on your life, career, relationships, etc.?

What can you do to help others facing a similar adversity?

How have you grown as a result of the adversity?

What can you do to reverse any negative impact on your life?

What can you do in the future to embrace and grow from this or other adversity?

CHOOSING DEVELOPMENT:

PERSONAL AND PROFESSIONAL

EFFECTIVENESS

> *"Our potential is one thing.*
> *What we do with it is quite another."*
> – Angela Duckworth

THE THOROUGHFARE OF LIFE

WHAT DOES IT MEAN to be highly effective? How does anyone develop the skills to become highly effective in achieving life and career goals? Let's look at some of what I call *"real-life examples,"* and then one example/idea of my own.

I think we can all agree on the concept that a Medal of Honor recipient is one the ultimate representations of effectiveness in the United States. The honor, after much scrutiny, is granted to any person who *"distinguishes himself or herself consciously by gallantry at the risk of life above and beyond the call of duty."* In order to receive the Medal of Honor, one has to have a clear mission, go above and beyond the call of duty, and overcome significant obstacles. My step great-grandfather, Archie Peck, was a Medal of Honor recipient for his bravery and valor in World War I. Archie, in spite of size *(he weighed 112 lbs. at the time)*, lost and surrounded by enemy, knew what his mission was and accomplished it.

Archie Peck

1894 – 1978

Medal of Honor Recipient

While serving as an infantryman in the United States Army 77th Division during the Meuse-Argonne Offensive of World War I, his unit found itself surrounded in the German lines. The unit would subsequently gain the moniker, *"The Lost Battalion,"* as a result of this incident. This was the bloodiest battle of the war involving U.S. troops. Private Peck acted gallantly while surrounded, saving two wounded men under machine gun fire. The citation read: *"While engaged with two other soldiers on patrol duty, he and his comrades were subjected to the direct fire of an enemy machine gun, at which time both his companions were wounded. Returning to his company, he obtained another soldier to accompany him to assist in bringing in the wounded men. His assistant was killed in the exploit, but he continued on, twice returning safely, bringing in both men, being under terrific machine-gun fire during the entire journey."*

Note: Archie returned from the war and settled in Western NY, had five sons, a successful career in the food industry, and lived to age 84. His oldest son, Robert, had two daughters, the younger being my step-mother.

Now let's move to another *real-life example*. Although there is no clear formula for winning a Nobel Prize, the award is generally granted to individuals who *"advance human knowledge"* and create solutions to the *"world's biggest problems"* while *"creating a paradigm shift."* In other words,

Nobel Prize recipients have distinguished themselves by accepting an inherently difficult and high standard full of obstacles *(the unknown)*.

Ralph Steinman, a 2011 Nobel Prize recipient who passed away from pancreatic cancer, *"was so engrossed in his cancer vaccine research that he developed and tested an experimental treatment on himself."* Throughout his career, Steinman significantly advanced medical science, going above and beyond the call of duty to do so.

Ralph Steinman
1943 – 2011
Noble Prize in Medicine Recipient

Dr. Steinman, a Canadian physician and medical researcher at Rockefeller University, discovered and named dendritic cells, receiving numerous awards and recognition for his lifelong work. Steinman's work advanced the field of immunology and the study and treatment of cancer and other diseases. A colleague stated: *"Ralph's research has laid the foundation for numerous discoveries in the critically important field of immunology, and it has led to innovative new approaches in how we treat cancer, infectious diseases, and disorders of the immune system."*

Note: Steinman died three days before the Nobel Prize was announced, which created a complication since the Nobel process stipulates that the award cannot be granted posthumously. An exception was made, and Steinman still received the award.

And then there are some other *real-life examples* of pure passion and persistence. A young journalist once challenged Thomas Edison saying to him, *"Mr. Edison, why do you keep trying to make light by using electricity when you have failed so many times? Don't you know that gas lights are with us to stay?"* To this Edison replied, *"Young man, don't you realize that I have not failed but have successfully discovered six thousand ways that won't work!"*

Once again, Edison accepted a nearly impossible mission exploring the scientific unknown with unimaginable persistence. He *"only"* had to get through six thousand obstacles on his way.

Thomas Edison
1847 – 1931
America's Greatest Inventor

Edison was an American inventor and businessman. He developed many devices in fields such as electric power generation, mass communication, sound recording, and motion pictures. And one can't forget, the long-lasting, practical, electric light bulb. He established the first industrial research laboratory and founded a company that later evolved into the General Electric Company. And, yes, it has been reported that Edison failed over 6,000 times before perfecting the first electric light bulb.

One last *real-life example...*

José Hernandez
Born August 7, 1962
NASA Astronaut

Hernandez grew up in a small town in California and worked alongside his family harvesting crops and moving from one town to another. He participated in an Upward Bound program in high school with preparation for college in science, technology, engineering, and math fields. He later received a bachelor of science degree in electrical engineering and a master's degree in computer science and engineering. Hernandez worked at the Lawrence Livermore National Laboratory and, along with a colleague, developed the first full-field digital mammography imaging system. After more than 20 years, he joined NASA in 2001 and became an astronaut in 2004. He was selected for a NASA Space Shuttle 14-day mission to the International Space Station that launched in 2009.

Hernandez's first memory of space was watching the Apollo 17 mission launch on television in 1972. He never lost his lifelong interest in becoming an astronaut and applied for astronaut training **eleven times** before being selected. Hernandez's life is the definition of passion and persistence.

Bottom line: Medal of Honor and Nobel Prize recipients, renowned inventors and astronauts, have set the bar extremely high and may have accomplishments that seem *"unreachable,"* but they have two common elements – a passion for extraordinary accomplishment *(going above and beyond),* and the ability and desire to persevere in spite of the obstacles *(whether physical, emotional, or mental).* All are requirements for the uncommon, highly effective mark.

THE PRESIDENT'S AWARD

Let's suppose you were selected to participate on a committee to develop the criteria for a new *"President's Award"* for your company. The award will be given annually to a deserving employee along with a significant monetary payment. *What would your criteria be in granting the award?*

You likely would start with those employees who are known for their impeccable character and who reflect positively on the organization. *(No jerks allowed.)* You might want to look for the most creative, innovative people who have developed new products and services or solved major problems. You likely would look for candidates who had good operational and/or financial results under difficult circumstances. You would look for people who were instrumental in improvement: product quality, efficient processes, cost savings, customer satisfaction. You likely would look for people who are on a mission *(the more difficult the better),* who are committed to accomplishing the goal *(i.e., they always finish)* and who enjoy the challenge of overcoming obstacles. You would look for people you respect.

So, *THAT* is my definition of highly effective. The development part is to ensure you have the skills necessary to be nominated for and receive the *"President's Award!"*

BUT FIRST, WHAT DO OTHERS SAY ABOUT EFFECTIVENESS?

There seems to have been more thought, study, research, writing, and speaking on *"how to improve your effectiveness"* than any other subject in the world. It is reported that *"self-help"* books are a billion-dollar genre.

Some self-help books over the last century seem to stand the test of time. My mission here was to look for common themes that at the very least would add some perspective and possibly add value regarding our choices and effectiveness paths that we choose. Although self-help books go back hundreds of years, we will start with *How to Win Friends and Influence People* by Dale Carnegie. The book was first published in 1936.

How to Win Friends... became an instant hit when it was published and remains popular to this day. The book made the Library of Congress list of *"books that shaped America."* The message is timeless with the main theme of getting what you want from others *(think customers buying your products, customers wanting your services, or your manager promoting you and recognizing your accomplishments)* by being genuinely interested in others, encouraging others to talk and then really listening, focusing on other's needs, acknowledging mistakes, and praising other's accomplishments *(no matter how small).* The advice is mostly simple things like remembering people's names, being nice, smiling a lot, asking people what you can do for them, and giving it to them or helping them get it in other ways. That really is a timeless list of advice.

The next popular self-help book that came along was more spiritually based: *The Power of Positive Thinking* by the famed clergyman, Norman Vincent Peale. The main theme is to banish negative thoughts *(that cause fear and failure)* and replace them with *"positive thinking."* Look forward... not backward; set goals for the future and work on them wholeheartedly and enthusiastically. If you fail, try again. Avoid obstacles when possible but, in any event, focus on solving problems. Peale's phrase: *"One never does wrong by doing right"* establishes the moral and ethical groundwork. Oh, and don't waste time by *"fuming and fretting." (I love this stuff.)*

And, then here comes Anthony (Tony) Robbins with several books, the first of which is *Unlimited Power*, published in 1986. The themes? Take control of your life, abolish your limitations, and achieve your most elusive goals. How? First, establish the values under which you will live. Then, build rapport and duplicate strategies of other successful people. Define what you want, identify what you need to get there, take action, and fine-tune your approach until you achieve your goals. There is a lot of Dale Carnegie and Norman Vincent Peale in Tony Robbins.

Likely the bestselling and most impactful self-help book in the last 30 years is *The 7 habits of Highly Effective People* by Stephen R. Covey. The first edition was published in 1989 and more than 25 million copies have been sold. Covey wraps the message into a seven can-do step process as a useful manual for self-improvement. Focus on character, not personality. You are what you do, so focus also on productive habits *(more to follow in the final chapter)*. Write a personal mission statement to clarify your principles and goals. Build trust in your relationships. Specifically, the seven habits are: be proactive, focus on goals, set appropriate priorities, think and act with others *(with win/win as the goal)*, communicate effectively *(understand and be understood)*, cooperate and synergize, and continuously improve *(reflect and repair deficiencies)*. The overall message of effectiveness is to know what you want to do and why you want to do it, develop your skills in order to do it, and will yourself to do it.

More recently is the *"Gladwellian"* approach to self-help based on the bestselling books of Malcolm Gladwell. Gladwell's books include *The Tipping Point* (2000), *Blink* (2005), and *Outliers* (2008). All deal with the sometimes unexpected implications of sociology and the psychology of human behavior. *Outliers: The Story of Success* popularized the *"10,000 Hour Rule"* – that building expertise takes 10,000 hours of practice. Gladwell cites examples where innate ability combined with a vision, dedication, and discipline leads to extraordinary performance and success. All books are based on common sense connections of sociological and psychological drivers.

Fast forward further to 2013 and Sheryl Sandberg. In her book, *Lean In*, she deals with developmental issues specifically for women *(although clearly they apply to everyone)* from the perspective of a successful corporate leader. In her book, she first documents the realities of the tensions between working and stay-at-home moms, the career penalties paid by women who devote time to their families, sexism in the workplace, differing benchmarks for evaluation of men and women, and the scarcity of women in senior positions in all types of organizations. However, in spite of the societal obstacles, Sandberg outlines a path for growth and development for women including:

- Using the normal female instincts of sensitivity and cooperation to their advantage by creating productive, collaborative work environments.

- Overcoming an often underestimation of abilities and value by making a concerted effort to *"speak up"* and make sure their voices are heard *(hence the title: Lean In)*.

- Letting go of the normal unconscious desire to be liked by everyone and become more issue driven.

- Discarding the image that there are two selves, the work self and the home self; embracing that the *authentic* self is the most effective self at home and at work.

- Emphasis on the importance of a partner who is supportive and who shares domestic responsibilities.

This chapter began by providing examples of several individuals who found their passion, persisted, and overcame obstacles. While the challenges of becoming highly effective apply to all, I believe they can be particularly challenging with the inherent work/life/family/societal issues affecting women. Ultimately, however, Sandberg advises women to find the balance that suits *YOU*.

Finally, if you are up for it, digest the 550-page treatise of Ray Dalio, *Principles of Life and Work.* I promise, you will be glad you did. Read the entire book or use it as a reference tool.

The book was published in 2017 and provides valuable insights for self-development, leadership, and organizational success. The book is organized in two main sections – life principles and work principles with a handy reference summary in the middle. Dalio's advice *(and there is plenty)* starts with *"whatever life you choose, make sure it fits your nature,"* and continues with *"make sure your work and your passion are one and the same."* There's much to be gained from the book, but Dalio's formula for success is summarily presented as a sequence of setting clear goals, welcoming challenges and addressing them, getting to the root cause of obstacles, creating detailed plans to fix problems, and doing whatever it takes to get results. The self-help suggestions are comprehensive and credible based on the business record and obvious thoughtfulness of the author.

All self-help gurus offer basic, good common sense advice with many common themes. But, now, let's get back on the development road to our *"President's Award..."*

WHAT IS ON THE ROAD TO THE PRESIDENT'S AWARD?

MILESTONE 1: Being self-aware *(knowing who you are).*

MILESTONE 2: Finding your passion.

MILESTONE 3: Fine-tuning your grit *(perseverance).*

MILESTONE 4: Becoming a problem solver.

MILESTONE 5: Focusing on the factors for earning respect.

MILESTONE 1: BE SELF-AWARE

Self-awareness is one of the most important skills for success. It is the anchor for making decisions about our jobs and careers and is the basis for determining our development needs. And self-awareness can be heightened in a number of ways.

In traditional organizations, the performance appraisal process will provide feedback regarding specific job performance. A 360-degree evaluation process may provide additional information from peers and subordinates. You may also be the instigator of surveys soliciting information about your interactions with others. Mentors *(formal or informal)* are a great source of feedback, as are family and friends. All will increase your self-awareness. But, also remember to always consider the validity and reliability of the source.

What about obtaining greater clarity about deeper issues – your values, your motivations, your broader strengths and weaknesses, your capabilities, and your career objectives? Remember Ray Dalio's advice: *"whatever life you choose, make sure it fits your nature"* and *"make sure your work and your passion are one and the same."* Dalio's further advice is to *"embrace reality and deal with it."* This can only be accomplished with open and honest self-analysis and awareness.

Exhibit II in the Appendix provides a list of questions that you might use for a basic self-assessment and may also be used to obtain feedback from others. Devise your own questions that will help you frame the issues that are important to you. If possible, compare your own self-assessment with the information provided by others.

Knowing your personality type will help you maximize your strengths, manage your weaknesses, and identify development plans. The commonly used Myers-Briggs Personality Type Indicator is a self-report indicator designed to identify a person's personality type. Although there are legitimate scientific issues regarding the test *(don't quit your day job based on the results)*, I believe the tool can be used to help people better understand themselves and potentially make better decisions as a result. If nothing else, it is a tool to open the dialog of self-awareness and reality *(a really good thing)*.

Another tool is a SWOT *(strengths, weaknesses, opportunities, and threats)* analysis originally designed as a strategic planning tool for organizations. The same concept can be applied as a tool for self-analysis. Strength and weakness focus on the individual *(internal factors)*, and opportunities and threats focus on the environment *(external factors)*. Yet another extremely useful tool for self-analysis, challenging us to look both inward and outward regarding our current qualities/ characteristics.

MILESTONE 2: FIND YOUR PASSION

Bill George, author of *Discover Your True North*, calls this the *"sweet spot."* He defines the sweet spot as: *"when you are good at what you are doing and fired up about doing it."*

Although I found my niche in college *(I loved accounting)*, my education evolved to an interest in auditing, which is where I began my career. I progressed in the traditional auditing field from an external audit staff *(I could write a whole book just about that experience)* to an Internal Audit Director. However, I could not see myself working in the corporate world forever with overly-defined structures and rigid processes. After leading and mentoring individuals in my Internal Audit Department, I became particularly interested in the education, training, and development of professionals as well as advancing new ideas for increasing the impact of internal audit on organizations. This was *(is)* my *"sweet spot,"* and in order to accomplish my goals, I started my own consulting business with an emphasis on education *(through both training and writing)* and new internal audit concepts and processes.

I performed my own self-assessment, and through additional assessment with family, friends, and colleagues, determined my *"true north,"* developed a plan to implement a pretty dramatic career change and pulled the trigger.

I believe I am good at what I do and I'm fired up about it *(Bill would be proud)*. All I can say is, follow the self-awareness steps and find your passion. I guarantee you will *only* earn the *"President's Award"* if you have passion about what you do.

MILESTONE 3: FINE-TUNE YOUR GRIT

Are you *"gritty"* in your personal and professional lives? What does being *"gritty"* mean? You may not know it, but your level of grit is likely correlated to your level of success. You have no chance of receiving the *"President's Award"* without it.

Angela Duckworth, a professor of psychology, wrote a compelling book, *Grit: The Power of Passion and Perseverance*. The book reports the results of systematic studies of characteristics of high achievers. Based on her studies, Professor Duckworth concluded that diligence and focus *(i.e., grit)* are more important than innate talent, aptitude, acquired skill, and education. She categorized grit into two components:

Passion: Working toward longer term goals with the necessary follow through to reach the goal, and

Perseverance: *Working with determination to stick with a project or problem in spite of obstacles until the work is done.*

Additional descriptive phases she uses to describe grit are: *never give up attitude, resilient, hardworking, determined, sense of direction, never discouraged, and maintaining continuity of interests.*

The world is a complicated place and every day it becomes more complicated. We established in the previous milestone that passion for what you do is critical to success. The additional element is *persistence,* further defined as:

➢ Focusing on what is important. Major on the majors. Don't nit-pick and get caught up in minutia.

➢ Setting stretch goals. Apply your full concentration and efforts to a key project or task.

➢ Committing to exceed expectations. Complete projects on time, every time, always following through.

➢ Being obsessed with adding value in everything you do. Make a permanent difference. Be the first to spot key improvement opportunities.

➢ Being highly efficient and cost effective in your efforts. Work smart and consistently get more done with fewer resources. And, continuously improve your skills and ability to make an impact.

➢ Building in contingency plans to ensure success. Be flexible; adjust actions based on changing conditions in order to reach the goal. Don't get distracted.

These are the gritty characteristics of high achievers as well as *"President's Award"* recipients.

So, how gritty are you? Professor Duckworth developed a test and a scale to measure your grit in order to determine your current level and compare your grit with others. The Grit Scale is available in Ms. Duckworth's book and on her website. I highly encourage all of you to read her book.

MILESTONE 4: BECOME A PROBLEM SOLVER

You don't have to be a Six Sigma Black Belt to have good problem-solving skills. But knowledge and understanding of Six Sigma concepts, tools, and techniques of problem-solving help. Successful organizations solve problems quickly and efficiently with permanent fixes. The best way to effectively contribute *(and win the "President's Award")* is to be the best, permanent problem-solver.

The original goal of Six Sigma was to provide the tools and techniques to improve the quality of products and services by controlling processes. The ultimate Six Sigma goal was to reduce error rates to no more than three defects per million parts. Many organizations that have embraced and fully implemented Six Sigma have achieved the goal. And those that are knowledgeable of the successful, problem-solving techniques are in a position to contribute their skills to improve organization effectiveness.

The Six Sigma core processes and tools for problem-solving are the following:

⇒ Process/Improvement Cycle (DMAIC) where problems are formally **D**efined, **M**easured to quantify the problem, **A**nalyzed to determine the root cause, and a solution selected and **I**mplemented with **C**ontrol testing to determine if the solution was effective.

⇒ <u>Quality Function Deployment (QFD)</u> where customer needs are systematically documented and prioritized to solve the most critical problems getting in the way.

⇒ <u>Failure Mode and Effects Analysis (FMEA)</u> where a follow up analysis is conducted to make sure solutions identified to solve problems do not cause collateral damage.

See the Choices workbook for my adapted version of these tools and forms to use in problem solving.

Highly effective people solve problems by identifying real, long-lasting or permanent solutions with no unintended consequences. I would add that they also actively participate in implementing the solutions. Find a big problem, solve it, engage in implementing the solution, and then nominate yourself for the *"President's Award."*

MILESTONE 5: FOCUS ON EARNING RESPECT

Can you imagine anyone receiving the *"President's Award"* that was not well-respected by others in the organization? While my *Respect Scale* may not be as scientific as the *Grit Scale* mentioned in Milestone 3, I believe rating yourself on certain criteria for earning respect can go a long way toward ensuring success. Henry Ford stated, *"you can't build a reputation on what you are going to do."* We will modify by stating, *"you can't earn respect based on what you are going to do."*

Have you ever heard someone say, *"I don't get any respect at my company,"* or have you ever said, *"I don't get any respect?"* If so, it is time to take a look at the respect criteria and see how you measure up.

Respect does not come from educational experience, professional credentials, or a reputation at previous employers.

Respect is derived directly from accomplishments and the following concepts and standards:

√ The path to respect in any profession begins with the understanding that respect is earned. There is nothing inherent about any one individual that deserves any special treatment, more than another.

√ You know you are contributing and earning respect when others seek out your counsel and contribution. My informal *Respect Scale* includes whether other individuals *"beat a path to your door" or "run the other way."*

√ You are assigned or volunteer for special projects that others do not want to do or cannot do.

√ You are known to independently *"deliver your function."* You set your own goals that support the organization and consistently meet or exceed your objectives. You need little direction.

√ You have a deep understanding of and belief in the overall organization's mission, values, and objectives.

√ You bring knowledge of best functional, business, and industry practices. You learn continuously.

√ You are genuinely customer focused and are known to constantly ask customers what you can do to help them achieve their goals. You care about the success of your customers and you fully understand their needs.

√ You do not waste time on things that don't count or don't help. You tackle high-risk, high-return projects and issues, and you help fix big problems.

√ You apply the latest tools and techniques of your function in order to be efficient and effective. You are known as the best _____ *(fill in your job title)* that the organizations has ever had.

√ You understand increased productivity is critical to success. You constantly look for ways to become more productive and help others do likewise.

√ You embrace change, offer suggestions for improvement, look for root causes, and recommend and implement permanent fixes.

√ You understand that professional characteristics are important. Your work is systematic, thorough, complete, and accurate.

√ You understand that personal characteristics are just as *(if not more)* important. You have impeccable character *(see the next chapter)* and are personable and approachable. You communicate well and listen often.

See Exhibit III in the Appendix for *The Respect Scale* to see where you stand. If your average rating is four or higher, you are a serious candidate for the *"President's Award."*

To conclude this rather lengthy chapter in a very brief way... the thoroughfare of life may be complex, but the development choices can be simple: become self-aware, find your passion, fine-tune your grit, improve your problem-solving skills, and focus on the factors in order to earn respect.

THIS IS THE DEVELOPMENT CHOICE.

"The best is for today; better is for tomorrow."
– John C. Maxwell

MY FAVORITE DEVELOPMENT QUOTES

"Make your passion and your work one and the same."
– Ray Dalio

"The future belongs to those who believe in the beauty of their dreams."
– Eleanor Roosevelt

"Success is not the key to happiness. Happiness is the key to success. If you love what you are doing, you will be successful."
– Albert Schweitzer

"The main thing is to keep the main thing the main thing."
– Steven Covey

"Success is the progressive realization of worthwhile, predetermined, personal goals."
– Paul Meyer

"Successful and unsuccessful people do not vary greatly in their abilities. They vary in their desire to reach their potential."
– John C. Maxwell

"I believe most people fail in life because they major on minor things."
– Anthony Robbins

"I do not think that there is any other quality so essential to success of any kind as the quality of perseverance. It overcomes almost everything, even nature."
– John D. Rockefeller

"What is necessary to change a person, is to change his awareness of himself."
– Abraham Maslow

EXPLORE YOUR DEVELOPMENT CHOICES.

How do you get honest feedback from others?

What IS the feedback you are getting from others?

What is your passion? What "fits your nature"? What is your "True North"?

What are the opportunities to pursue your passions in your current "life" state?

What are your strengths?

How can you build them to become more highly effective (think of the milestones)?

What are your weaknesses?

How can you overcome them to become more highly effective (again, think of the milestones)?

What are your plans for self-development and effectiveness-building?

CHOOSING IMPECCABLE CHARACTER:

BECOMING THE EVERYDAY ETHICIST

> *"What does it all mean*
> *if there is no honor and character?"*
> – John Bogle

CROSSROADS OF LIFE

RESEARCHERS PLANTED MORE than 17,000 lost wallets across 355 cities in 40 countries and kept track of how many *"finders"* contacted the owner. Fifty-one percent did. *Would you?* I know, you immediately cannot even believe I would ask you this question. But, remember 49% didn't.

National surveys have reported that over 50% of graduate students across all fields of study *(e.g., business, law, engineering, education)* admit to cheating on exams. Researchers also suggest since the data is based on self-reporting, the number is probably underestimated. And studies show that test participants are more likely to cheat when paid for performance, particularly when there is no way to detect the cheating.

Big Four auditors *(including partners)* were complicit in using stolen information to gain a competitive advantage. And when ethics and integrity training was mandated by a regulatory agency, cheating in various forms on the *ETHICS* training was discovered.

The *"founding father"* of research regarding academic integrity, Donald McCabe of Rutgers University, has observed that there is a generation that has an attitude of indifference to cheating. McCabe reports that students have a *"willing to do anything to get the job done"* attitude and outlook.

So, with all this in mind, think about how you would honestly rate your ethics? I believe our personal ethics *(and in turn our overall character)* is tested daily in many ways... ways that can seem small or inconsequential, but, in reality, can have a big impact.

For instance, you're at the store and the cashier forgets to ring up a $2.00 item. *Do you say something?* Or do you let it go... thinking, it's only a couple bucks. Same scenario except now your bank statement shows a $2,000 deposit and you only deposited $1,000. *Now, do you say something?*

Do you put a price tag on your ethics? Or do you act with integrity at any cost?

John Bogle
1929 – 2019
American businessman, financial innovator, philanthropist
Founder of the world's largest mutual fund company, Bogle became interested in the investment industry in the 1950s. He selected a study of the industry as the topic for his college thesis. After conducting his statistical research, he discovered that mutual funds *"can make no claim"* (which they were doing

then and now) over long-term market averages and that fees associated with investing *only* negatively affect investor returns. To Bogle, this was an ethical and character issue. After ongoing study and years of experience in the investment business having difficulty beating market averages, he founded the Vanguard Group of mutual funds. The new *"mutual"* company put the interests of investors ahead of the fund managers and traders by focusing on index funds and low fees – honestly serving the needs and desires of investors.

John Bogle was tested and chose the side of honor and character *(a rare quality in the financial services industry)*, not the side of financial self-interest.

Harriet Tubman
1822 – 1913
Civil war scout, spy, nurse, civil rights activist

Harriett Tubman *(born Araminta Ross)* was born into slavery and became an American abolitionist and political activist. Tubman escaped slavery and subsequently led numerous rescue missions to free enslaved people, family, and friends, as well as helping newly freed slaves find work. During the American Civil War, she first served as a cook and a nurse, then as an armed scout and spy for the United States Army. Tubman was the first woman to lead an armed expedition in the war and she guided a raid that led to the liberation of more than 700 slaves. In her later years, Tubman was an activist in the struggle for women's rights.

Harriet Tubman is an icon of courage and freedom, and whenever tested, she landed squarely on the side of *doing the right thing* even in the face of great personal danger.

SO, WHY UNETHICAL CONDUCT?

Some seem to be oblivious to right and wrong as Professor McCabe observed. Some *(many)* are motivated by greed. Some are motivated by personal glory and power. Some place relationships above character. Some place their job above their character. Some cannot handle conflict of any sort nor the difficult choices thrown at us over a lifetime. And some simply rationalize away any personal responsibility in unethical conduct.

THE BIG ME

David Brooks in his bestselling book, *The Road to Character*, introduced the concept of the *"The Big Me."* To simplify, Brooks sees an ongoing sociological shift from a society that emphasized the integrity and trust of the individual to a society of individuals who are much more selfish, materialistic, and narcissistic. The top American scandals in the last several decades provide supporting evidence.

To me, the college admissions scandal *(uncovered in 2019)* is the classic example. There is really no other explanation than the desire to perpetuate the *big me* of those who bribed for their *future big me's* benefit.

Then, looking back in time, there were *"the smartest guys in the room"* who committed fraud and bankrupted Enron along with *the smartest auditors in the room* who were self-serving and ruined Arthur Anderson. All for power, prestige, and personal gain.

There was the chief executive officer (CEO) at Tyco International and his extravagant lifestyle *(all charged to the company, of course)* until he went to jail for fraud.

There were executives at Volkswagen who perpetrated a huge emissions scandal all for the power and prestige of achieving market share leadership.

There was the negligence and willful poor safety conduct at BP that led to the largest environmental disaster in history, all for greater profits.

The list continues... the recklessness of executives at Lehman Brothers that contributed to the 2008 financial crisis, the greed of branch employees at all levels at Wells Fargo to earn incentives by fraudulently opening customer accounts, and let's not forget the power and prestige motives and greed that fueled Bernie Madoff.

Oh, and a little known but excellent *big me* case study of the CEO of General Electric, who selfishly directed an empty corporate jet follow his personal jet on a worldwide trip, *just in case* there was a mechanical failure.

Accounting scandals of overstating earnings, cases of financial engineering, falsification of financial statements, underreporting costs, and just plain making up numbers, mostly to fuel stock prices and pump up personal bonuses... the *big me* in action in corporate America.

From the 49% that did not return the wallet to the 50% that cheated on graduate school exams... to the individuals and executives at the aforementioned organizations... there is a whole lot of *big me* going on out there.

Brook's message, agree or not, is that *"people are more isolated, less likely to have empathy for others, and in general, less oriented to things like community."* People today *"lack the ability to articulate and engage in moral reasoning...."*

And, as John Bogle has stated, *"it's amazing how difficult it is for a man to understand something if he's paid a small fortune not to understand it."* This comment applies particularly well for some of the *big me's* mentioned above. *Don't you agree?*

The point... Don't be a *big me*. Don't work for a big me organization or boss.

Quit your job, before you quit your ethics.

I did once.

Hands down, the best decision I ever made.

THE ETHICAL RATIONALIZERS

Almost every book on ethics talks about the impact of rationalization on ethical conduct. Dr. McCabe's graduate students claimed, *"everyone was cheating"* and *"cheating was necessary to get ahead,"* as a rationalization for their actions.

I'll bet that most who did not return the *"lost"* wallet rationalized by saying to themselves: *"Not my fault; I didn't lose the wallet,"* or *"I bet if I lost my wallet, no one would return it."* My guess is that the 50% who cheated on the exams also wouldn't return the wallet...

Psychological research clearly shows that we are not as ethical as we think we are. Sometimes we are conscious of our unethical conduct, but sometimes we are not.

Studies consistently show that we have the capability to behave contrary to our best intentions. We have an ability *(if you can call it an ability)* to maintain a belief, while simultaneously acting contrary to it. We are often hypercritical, judging others more harshly than ourselves when evaluating the same transgressions. There is often a widespread double standard – one set of rules for ourselves, one set of rules for others. The conclusion is that the subject of behavioral ethics is complex. *There is no easy fix.*

For a comprehensive view of ethics, read *Blind Spots* by Max H. Bazerman and Ann E. Tenbrunsel. Bazerman and Tenbrunsel have engaged in extensive research, writing, teaching, and consulting in the area of business ethics.

The purpose of this book is not to try to turn everyone into ethics gurus. My book, *Becoming The Everyday Ethicist,* does that. The purpose of this section is, however, to raise the awareness of the causes of unethical conduct. The causes can be neatly categorized and, I would argue, most are obvious. Many involve some sort of rationalization for the unethical behavior.

The classic rationalization case comes from the former chief financial officer (CFO) at Enron. Even though the facts clearly show rampant accounting fraud for which he was convicted *(and went to prison),* the former CFO claimed that in part he felt the actions were justified *(rationalized)* because the attorneys and auditors at the time approved the actions. This is not an acceptable rationalization *(if there is such a thing).* Trust your own instincts first; do not rely on *(or blame)* others.

An even simpler example of business rationalization? People will engage in unethical behavior in order to fulfill formal or informal obligations to authority. *"My boss told me to do it."* Can you think of situations where ethical considerations were compromised to satisfy your boss or members of your management? *I can.* I lived it for a very short period of time before choosing my new career path.

Often cited in discussions of ethics is the 1986 Challenger space shuttle failure. There was evidence of potential O-ring failure at low temperatures *(and there were unprecedented low temperatures on the morning of the launch).* But pressure from NASA *(the customer in this case)* to launch trumped the judgement of Morton Thiokol engineers who recommended not to launch. Again, can you think of situations where ethical considerations were compromised to satisfy others, whoever they may be?

Group think, *"a tendency for cohesive groups to avoid a realistic appraisal of an alternative course of action in favor of unanimity,"* can result in unethical conduct. The group think environment sometimes prevents individuals *(or small groups)* from challenging questionable, unethical decisions. I bet you can think of an example where you went along with the crowd and regretted it later *(think high school y'all – everyone is doing it. Yes, I went to high school in the South).*

And there is unambiguous evidence of the psychological aspects of conflicts of interest. Consider a typical cancer patient who receives advice from three prominent physicians, representing three specialties in cancer treatment: a surgeon, a radiologist, and a homeopathic physician. Would anyone be surprised that the respective physicians recommended a treatment protocol that was consistent with their area of specialization only?

The financial services industry is *full* of conflict situations. Are financial advisors and brokers looking out for investor interests or their own? What is their rationalization? I know I gave poor advice, but the customer/investors would have made even worse decisions on their own. *(Pure hogwash.)*

There is always a rationalization for acting in a self-serving, sometimes unethical, manner. Training, incentives, and personal preferences sometimes prevent objectivity and create an ethical dilemma.

Most of us behave ethically, *most* of the time. But very few of us behave ethically, *all* of the time. Some people rationalize so much that they don't recognize an ethical dilemma for what it is. In fact, at times we are completely oblivious to ethical considerations. We have *"blind spots" (again, see the Bazerman and Tenbrunsel book).*

We all have different life experiences. Money, authority, customers, peers, groups, and a multitude of conflicts of interest situations can lead to lack of objectivity *(blind spots)* resulting in unethical conduct.

We rationalize behavior and tend to ignore future consequences of our actions, particularly if there is no perceived or actual harm at the time. Also, environments with questionable ethics can easily perpetuate unethical conduct *(ethical and moral relativism).* We rationalize and simply call the unethical decision a *"business decision."* Sadly, a quite common rationalization.

Finally, self-preservation can be the biggest rationalizer of them all and can easily overwhelm ethical considerations. Would you quit your job before doing something unethical? Or are you in the *"I thought I would lose my job"* rationalization camp? These are important questions you need to consider.

THE EVERYDAY ETHICIST

What is the road to becoming the everyday ethicist? *I'm glad you asked.* The road of the everyday ethicist is one where we *only* make ethical decisions. It is a road where we make decisions that are the result of thoughtful, reasoned reflection of our personal values. And it is a road where we do what *should* be done... a road where we do no harm to others.

It may sound simple, but the truth is it takes hard work. That is why *"character"* choices are the most important choices that we will ever make. *Here are the choices:*

❖ Recognize that everyone *(I mean everyone)* is vulnerable to unethical behavior.

❖ Develop your personal value statement and code of conduct as your guide.

❖ Practice writing down thoughts to get a clear, developed plan for conduct and actions.

❖ Visualize defending your actions in front of a judge or arbitrator.

❖ Imagine an article on the front page of the Wall Street Journal describing your actions and determine if you would be comfortable defending those actions to your pastor, priest or rabbi, parents, or children.

❖ Project ethical challenges into future situations and pre-commit to intended ethical choices.

❖ Judge your own ethical decisions the way you would judge others – which is by their *behavior (not their intentions).*

❖ Review critical ethical decisions and alternative actions with personal mentors or professional colleagues/trusted advisors before acting.

❖ Make decisions as if you had trusteeship, stewardship, or fiduciary responsibility *(whether legally required or not)* for the best interest of those impacted by your decisions.

❖ Meet or exceed your commitments but do not overcommit or exaggerate. Be fact driven. *It is much better if the truth beats what you say than if what you say falls short of the truth.*

❖ Professional conduct is defined as *"a commitment to the interests of clients (stakeholders), in particular, and society, in general."* Any conflicts between professional *(ethical)* conduct and business conduct must be reconciled in favor of the stakeholders *(professional conduct).*

❖ Think of your actions in a *"it's my own business"* context. Customers do not want to do business with an organization they do not trust; employees do not want to work for an organization they do not trust; investors do not want to invest in an organization they do not trust.

❖ Don't let an ethical challenge go to waste. Let every ethical crisis develop your character and strengthen your resolve to do the right thing.

❖ Be proud of your integrity; be a model for ethical conduct; walk the talk and encourage and inspire others to do likewise.

❖ Build your most important ethical assets of courage, honesty, and humility. Your ego is what will lead to your downfall. Courage, honesty, and humility never will *(thank you, David Brooks).*

See Exhibit IV in the Appendix for my *Everyday Ethicist Contract.* Print it, post it, live by it.

Unfortunately, most people spend their life focusing on *"resume virtues"* – education and skill development to make money and advance our careers. It is now time to focus on our *"eulogy virtues"* – qualities that will endure forever more *(again, thank you, David Brooks).* It is time to focus on the Bogle and Tubman character and courage traits within us.

And, when you come to the crossroads of life where you must choose the road of ethical conduct vs. unethical conduct... choose to say something, *even if...*

Even if... it only costs two dollars.

Even if... it costs you a friend.

Even if... it costs you your job.

THIS IS THE CHARACTER CHOICE.

"Truth is the only ground to stand on."
– Elizabeth Cady Stanton

MY FAVORITE CHARACTER QUOTES

"Ethical decisions ensure that everyone's best interests are protected. When in doubt, don't."
– Harvey Mackay

"We become just by doing just actions."
– Aristotle

"Ethics is a code of values which guide our choices and actions and determine the purpose and course of our lives."
– Ayn Rand

"Education without values, as useful as it is, seems rather to make man a more clever devil."
– C.S. Lewis

"Ethics is knowing the difference between what you have a right to do and what is right to do."
– Potter Stewart

"To care for anyone else enough to make their problems one's own, is ever the beginning of one's real ethical development."
– Felix Adler

"Ethics is about how we meet the challenge of doing the right thing, when that will cost more than we want to pay."
– The Josephson Institute of Ethics

"Ethics is not a description of what people do; It's a prescription for what we all should do."
– Michael Josephson

"The way to gain a good reputation is to endeavor to be what you desire to appear."
– Socrates

EXPLORE YOUR CHARACTER CHOICES.

What are the core values that define your life?

What values do you believe have contributed to your successes?

What values (ignored) contributed to your adversity?

What are the core values that got you through adversity?

Give examples where the "the big me" mentality (personally or by others) has affected you.

Give examples where you failed to live up to your values by rationalizing.

What are your ethical boundaries?

At what point will you quit your job, get out of a relationship, etc., before you quit your ethics?

How can you handle situations in the future when you fear a compromise in your values?

What is your character development plan for your future?

Choosing an Owner Mentality:

An Entrepreneurial Spirit

> *"Do every job you're in like you're going to do it*
> *for the rest of your life, and*
> *demonstrate ownership for it."*
> – Mary Barra

Boulevard of Dreams

JUST FOR CLARITY, when I write about *"entrepreneurship"* and *"ownership,"* I don't mean you have to go out and start your own company. The question is whether you *"think and act"* like an entrepreneur and *"think and act"* like an owner.

I am attempting to describe the thoughts: the passion, the outlook, the attitude, and the emotional rewards, as well as the actions: innovation, risk-taking, dedication, and work ethic of an owner. In my opinion, all of the listed qualities and characteristics *(and more)* will serve you well in whatever you do. With that in mind, we will now travel down the *"boulevard"* of the entrepreneurial spirit and ownership mentality, regardless of your current occupation.

My comments are based on my observations and experiences as a professional in corporate America and owner of a small consulting firm. Whether you are an individual contributor, team leader, manager, or executive, I believe the messages apply.

First, I suggest that you think of your current job as your own professional service firm. You are now the founder and sole owner of...

MY JOB, LLC

What would be the driving values and objectives of your company? What would you want to provide to your customers? What would you want your customers to say about you and your services? Would you do anything differently as a professional service provider at My Job, LLC?

I expect, as a successful entrepreneur and business owner of My Job, LLC, you would want to build a successful brand and positive reputation *(your future business is at stake)*. The focus would be entirely on creating and providing high-quality, valuable services to customers *(your income is at stake)*. You would listen to your customers' needs in detail *(your future relationship and, again, your income are at stake)*. You would be 100% engaged treating each customer as if they were your first *(and as they might be your last)*.

You would likely want to build a personal and professional connection so there is a strong bond with the customer. Everything would be a collaborative process between what the customer needs and what value you can provide. You would be committed to creating positive change, since you will be acting on the needs of the customer, and the customer has undoubtedly hired you to change or improve something. You understand if the customer succeeds, your business succeeds. And, you will always be interested in reaching new customers to expand your impact *(and income)*.

You will likely go above and beyond the customers' expectations and are hopeful that your customers will tell their colleagues what excellent work you are doing for them. You will not waste your customers' or your own time *(your reputation and profitability are at stake)*.

Your customers' perspective is simple. They want to contract services from someone who can identify and implement solutions to problems, improve processes, and answer the *"why,"* not just the *"what"* happened, questions. They want someone who is open, honest, and transparent and who performs superb work in a timely, efficient manner. They don't want *"nit pickers"* that point out *"small potatoes."* They want a material impact out of the work performed. They want a collaborative effort to accomplish the goal. *Period.*

Are you performing your job as if you are a professional services provider, the founder and owner of My Job, LLC?

Are you functioning with an entrepreneurial spirit and an owner's mentality?

ENTREPRENEURIAL SPIRIT AND OWNERSHIP MENTALITY: DEFINED

Having an *"entrepreneurial spirit"* means looking at the world in a different way. It is an idea. It is having a vision. It is a mindset of change. It is an attitude of finding new ways to do things. It is willingly diving into the unknown, learning at high speed, being flexible, building new relationships, and selling yourself. The outcome: *Unbelievable personal satisfaction.*

Having an *"owner's mentality"* also means looking at the world in a different way. It is being frugal and at the same time making risky investments. It is being innovative and practical. It is *"out of the box"* thinking while not forgetting common sense. It is always doing more than expected, it is treasuring your customers and understanding their needs, and it is continuously improving what you do every day. The outcome? *Unbelievable personal satisfaction.*

Both sets of descriptions often run counter to large, bureaucratic organizations. Ironically, most would love to be described in this way. Just another reason why putting these descriptions in action will serve you well, wherever you are.

ENTREPRENEURIAL SPIRIT AND OWNERSHIP MENTALITY: IN ACTION

The following are *"tips"* to apply your *entrepreneurial spirit* and *ownership mentality* for greater success, in whatever you do. The tips are, more or less, listed in the order I believe appropriate to travel the path to success.

Remember, regardless of the environment, everyone is a customer to someone and supplier to someone.

TIP NUMBER 1:

Be infinitely self-aware then pursue your passion. (This should sound familiar.) In the chapter dedicated to Self-Development, I wrote *"self-awareness is one of the most important skills for success. It is the anchor for making decisions about our jobs and careers."* I further wrote that it is necessary *"to find your passion to succeed."* Having an *entrepreneurial spirit* and an *ownership mentality* starts with serious thinking about what you hope to have and do. Then you do the basic planning to get there and leap into execution. *All successful roads (or "boulevards of dreams") start here.*

TIP NUMBER 2:

Plan the basics then be a doer. Don't worry about grandiose plans but respect the planning process. Dwight Eisenhower said, *"Plans are useless, but planning is indispensable."* This applies to enterprises as well as individual contributors. Focus your energy, take action, market your idea, and see if it works. Organizations of all sizes are always in need of doers because organizations and enterprises most often fail because of lack of execution *(not lack of planning). Be a doer. Get moving. And, be prepared to work hard.*

TIP NUMBER 3:

Selling equals trust and trust equals selling. People buy things and engage services from people they trust. People are trusted because they have a record of honesty, integrity, character, and fair play. Believe in and behave as *"a promise is a promise"* when it comes to your commitments. How people get an opportunity *(as long as it is ethical)* doesn't matter as much as what a person does when the opportunity presents itself. What matters is your performance. *Always do the right thing.*

TIP NUMBER 4:

Engage your customers. Every opportunity you get, interact with your customers and potential customers. Listen to your customers. If you are really good, and you listen well, your customers will tell you exactly what they want from you and they will even tell you how you can benefit from them. Early on, I had a customer tell me that I was not charging enough, explaining that I was as good *(if not better)* than many others providing similar services. I took it as an extreme compliment, and I listened and raised my prices shortly thereafter! And this doesn't just apply to entrepreneurs. In a corporate environment, you can judge your performance by whether customers seek you out for your advice, counsel, and services, and whether they provide guidance to you along the way as well. *Speak to and listen to everyone. Everyone is now your customer.*

TIP NUMBER 5:

Pay the price of entrepreneurship. I have given away countless books *(my own and others)* and given many complimentary speeches and seminars. It helped me improve my speaking skills, established relationships, provided exposure to my books and ideas and, in some cases, provided an opportunity for me to give back to the community for a good cause. *(I hope I'm in a position to give back indefinitely.)* Go above and beyond the *"call of duty"* even if it is not *"in your budget"* or *"normal"* schedule. In a corporate environment, look for ways to go outside of your normal responsibilities by volunteering for special projects and assignments. Not *just* focusing on the paycheck, may just bring even *more* of a paycheck *(when you least expect it)*. *Focus on the job you're doing, not the money you are making, no matter your environment.*

TIP NUMBER 6:

Add value and solve problems. Focus on the reason you exist. Look for better ways. Develop your product and/or service making sure it adds value to your potential or existing customers. As Guy Kawasaki writes in his book, *Wise Guy,* *"It's easy to get people excited about a great product; it's hard to get people excited about crap."* Be prepared to respond to unforeseen circumstances, new developments, and changes to reality. Nimble, flexible problem-solvers are always in demand, everywhere, corporate environments included. No matter where you are, do what Tom Peters says... *"make the work matter."*

TIP NUMBER 7:

Be the expert then be innovative and unique. What are you an expert in/at? What is unique about you and/or your product or services? What can you do that's the best in the world? *(Aim high. Now, aim even higher.)* How do you provide something that creates excitement and motivates your customers to want more and tell others? Create products and services that are more innovative and unique, not just in small ways, *in big ways.* Success is when customers beat a path to your door. Know your competitors and think about your competitive advantage. This works whether you are an entrepreneur or in a corporate environment. *Just stand out.*

TIP NUMBER 8:

Design and presentation make a difference. Have innovative designs and presentations that are absolute *"killers."* For example, I get lots of compliments on my multi-media presentations. *And guess what?* Presentation creativity is free. So, get good at it! Build creative designs into all that you do. And while we are on the subject, take pride in how you look as well. Dress for the job you *want*, not the job you *have. (I could write a book on this as well.)* I am not saying you have to go out and buy a new wardrobe or hire a designer *(for your presentations OR you),* but take a long look in the mirror and see if there is anything that could make you stand out. *First impressions are real. Presentation matters.*

TIP NUMBER 9:

Build good relationships. Your reputation will precede you on your way to your customers, suppliers, and associates. *"It's not who you know; it's who knows you" (thank you for the reminder, Guy Kawasaki).* Make all your interactions clear, to the point yet comprehensive, easy to understand, honest, and kind. Interact with people even if you disagree or see little immediate opportunity, because the more exposure, the greater the possibility of finding a mutual interest and opportunity for collaboration. Pretend that every single person you meet has a sign around his or her neck that says, *"make me feel important" (thank you, Stephen Covey).* Because, they should all be important to *you. Relationships matter. People matter.*

TIP NUMBER 10.

Be thoroughly professional. Have a clear picture of what you represent. Have a purpose. Develop your own values and mission statement to show your customers and associates, as well as to remind yourself daily. Always put your customers first and look out for their interests, even above your own. Have unwavering integrity. Be an everyday ethicist *(again, this should sound familiar. Repetition is the key to learning.)* And have checks and balances to ensure that you deliver on all your promises. Make quick, meaningful decisions and create a sense of urgency. These concepts are universally applicable. *If there are no fires burning, light a few. Ethically, of course.*

TIP NUMBER 11:

Collaborate with quality. If you have partners and/or associates in your efforts, make sure their roles and contributions are well defined and add as much value to the enterprise as you do.

Winners pick winners for their team. Don't compromise. In a corporate environment, surround yourself with *"aces"* – people who are equal to or better than you are and bring specific expertise. The people around you must be *"true believers"* in what you are trying to accomplish. They must have common hopes and ambitions. Those you associate with are your *"brand."* Make sure they have an *entrepreneurial spirit,* an *ownership mindset,* and are determined to make a difference *(like you).* And make sure you all <u>never</u> <u>stop</u> <u>learning</u> *(back track to the Self-Development chapter).*

TIP NUMBER 12:

Ensure the economics make sense. Ensure the startup investments and costs make economic sense to the enterprise or organization *(whether yours or someone else's)* relative to the value that is added to customers. If you start a business, strive to provide valuable products and services customers need *(and will pay for).* If you start a new position, make sure your contribution more than justifies your cost. If you lead a team or department, make sure the value added by your group is greater than the cost. If you lead a profit center, make sure you make a profit! *After all, business is still business.*

TIP NUMBER 13:

Understand the difference between price and value. Let your exceptional value drive the price. *My example?* I sell trainings *(my time),* but I also provide both my book and workbook *(what I see as an even greater value)* to every participant *(i.e., the customer).* This additional value justifies the price/cost and, of course, provides me a revenue premium. In a corporate environment, over the long term, *your value is always directly proportional to your contribution.* If it doesn't work, find a way to increase your contribution, or find another place to work where your contribution is appropriately valued. *Value matters first.*

TIP NUMBER 14:

Pay it forward. From the beginning of my business, I have offered a free consultation for any subject, for any reason. The typical response is one of appreciation and disbelief *(apparently few offer free consultations in my industry).* All I can say is, nothing but good things have come from these free consultations. And, believe it or not, pay it forward does work just as well in a corporate environment. Look for opportunities to contribute above and beyond the norm... to help other colleagues, departments, or teams. Volunteer outside of work hours. Find a passion in giving back to the community or to your industry or profession. Join an association. Join a board. *The upside always far outweighs the downside (if there really even is a downside).*

****

See Exhibit V in the Appendix for a summary of the *14 Tips for Successful "Owners" of their Life.* Print it, post it, live by it. *Your career will thank you.*

In his book, *Shortcut to Prosperity*, Mark Hopkins describes a *"prosperity cycle... take a chance, work hard, win, gain confidence, take another chance, work hard, win, gain confidence, win again."* It has worked for me. It worked when I was in a corporate setting and it works for me as a business owner and entrepreneur.

No matter what you do, choose to take your *entrepreneurial spirt* and your *owner mentality* with you. Be a good person, who helps others, does what's right, and pays something back to society. Think about the legacy that you are creating. How do you want to be remembered? As someone who lived, worked, and lead as an *owner* and *entrepreneur* of their own life? That's about as good as it gets on the *boulevard of dreams*.

THIS IS THE OWNERSHIP AND ENTREPRENEURIAL CHOICE.

"Whatever you are, be a good one."
– Abraham Lincoln

MY FAVORITE OWNERSHIP QUOTES

"I knew that if I failed I wouldn't regret that, but I knew the one thing I might regret is not trying."
– Jeff Bezos

"Always deliver more than is expected."
– Larry Page

"In the end, people buy from people."
– Subroto Bagchi

"Timing, perseverance and 10 years of trying will eventually make you look like an overnight success."
– Biz Stone

"It's fine to celebrate success but it is more important to heed the lessons of failure."
– Bill Gates

"Logic will get you from A to B. Imagination will take you everywhere."
– Albert Einstein

"Success is not what you have, but who you are."
– Bo Bennet

"When you find an idea that you just can't stop thinking about, that's probably a good one to pursue."
– Josh James

*"To be a star, you must shine your own light,
follow your own path,
and don't worry about darkness,
for that is when the stars shine brightest."*
– Napoleon Hill

EXPLORE YOUR OWNER MINDSET AND ENTREPRENEURIAL CHOICES.

Who are your customers?

How well do you know your customers?

What can you do to build a better relationship with your customers?

Describe the problems and issues that your customers are having in reaching their goals?

What methods could you use to better understand your customers' problems in reaching their objectives?

Do your capabilities and skills match the needs of your customers? What are your corrective action plans if they don't?

Describe your innovative and unique ideas and plans to better meet the needs of your customers?

How will you know if you are meeting the needs of your customers?

How are you standing out?

How are you "paying it forward?"

What is your action plan to have an entrepreneurial spirit and an ownership mentality?

CHOOSING GENUINE LEADERSHIP:

LEADERSHIP CHARACTER COUNTS, TWICE

"The greatest leaders we've studied throughout all our research cared as much about values as victory, as much about purpose as profit, and as much about being useful as being successful."
– Jim Collins

STEADY ON THE RIDE

AS YOU READ THIS CHAPTER, think of leadership in the broadest sense. You can be a board member, an executive, a member of middle management... a front-line supervisor, a project manager, a team captain, or an individual contributor that simply interacts with others... and you are a leader. In all cases, you affect others and the messages and pitfalls are the same. As Bill George states in his book, *The True North Fieldbook*, *"any time you face a decision that impacts others, you are leading."* But to start the leadership character conversation, let's discuss a few *"leaders"* you might know.

LEADERSHIP CASE STUDIES

I have a friend who once worked for a successful *"turnaround"* executive *(i.e., the CEO)*. Under very difficult financial circumstances *(near bankruptcy)*, the new CEO quickly re-set the company mission, strategy, and tactics. The CEO had a charisma that *"rallied the troops"* toward putting forth necessary extreme effort. The CEO made the tough short-term cost cutting financial decisions, while at the same time having the vision to make strategic long-term investments that were necessary to support long-term viability. He negotiated necessary company saving short-term pay reductions with the local union. He led the efforts to renegotiate financial arrangements that ensured the resources necessary to support the turnaround efforts. He led necessary organization changes and recruited new, more efficient staff. He instituted operational and process changes that were brilliant and effective. In other words, the CEO saved the company and the jobs of those who *"survived."* But, here's the catch. *(I know you were waiting for it.)* The CEO was a bully, profane, an egomaniac, sexist, rude to the point of abusive, and the list of unsavory characteristics goes on endlessly. He famously stated in an *"all hands"* meeting, *"I hear some of you are unhappy working here; do me a favor and leave."* So, I ask you:

Was the turnaround executive REALLY an effective leader?

****

Bobby Knight, the legendary basketball coach at Indiana University, was one of the *"winningest"* coaches in college basketball history with three national championships. But he has been publicly described as a *"classic bully"* who has physically abused players, engaged in shoving matches and verbal confrontations with fans, frequently cursed at one and all, and received countless technical fouls and fines. So, I ask you:

Was Bobby Knight REALLY an effective leader?

****

We all know the innovative brilliance of Steve Jobs, the founder of Apple, who simply needs no other introduction. Jobs has been described as a classic narcissist with a rude and abrasive personality who yelled at colleagues when things did not go well and cared more about himself and his company than others. So, I ask you:

Was Steve Jobs REALLY an effective leader?

Read the book, *Steve Jobs,* by Walter Isaacson before you answer.

****

Martin Winterkorn was elevated to the position of CEO of Volkswagen (VW) in 2007 after leading the Audi subsidiary in a successful effort to challenge BMW in market share. Winterkorn implemented a strategy to take on Toyota's world dominance by introducing improved marketing, product design, and operations. He achieved the goal of attaining the leading market share in 2015. Winterkorn also set extremely unrealistic objectives that are widely considered to be the fuel that led to a culture that instigated a massive fraud of world-wide emissions regulations. So, I ask you:

Was Winterkorn REALLY an effective leader?

****

Now come the *real* questions. What did the Athletic Director and Board of Directors of Indiana University think of Bobby Knight as a leader? And how would you assess their leadership skills in allowing the abusive and inappropriate behavior to continue for so many years before corrective action was taken? (*Knight was fired in 2000 after coaching for 29 years at IU.*)

What did the Board of Directors of Apple think of Steve Jobs' leadership skills? And, what do you think of the Board's leadership skills in the way they handled Steve Jobs' behavior? (*Jobs was terminated in 1985 and re-hired in 1997 and continued employment at Apple until he died in 2011.*)

What did the Board of VW think of the culture that was created at VW under the leadership of Winterkorn? What do you think of the leadership of the Board in allowing a culture to persist that ultimately lead to such a massive fraud? *(Winterkorn resigned (i.e., fired) in 2015 in the middle of the emissions fraud scandal.)*

Good people who are leaders sometimes get good results. Sometimes good people get poor results. The unfortunate and confusing thing about leadership is that really bad people sometimes get good results. So, in my opinion *(likely not shared by all)*, it is not a question about whether you get results; it is a question of how you do it. In *genuine* leadership, the ends do not justify the means. The *genuine* leadership mission is not, *"get the results at all cost." Genuine* leaders don't just care about where you are going, they also care about *how* you get there.

As John Bogle said, *"What does it all mean if there is no honor and character?"* What are winning, innovation, and market share when there is abuse, narcissistic behavior, and dishonesty?

Just like the subject of self-help, everyone has an opinion on effective leadership. And, countless books and articles have been written on the subject. Sorting through the meaningful and *"not so much"* is actually quite easy. There are six individuals that stand out for their decades of practical experience, thoughtfulness, research, and writing regarding effective leadership. They are Peter Drucker, Warren Bennis, Bill George, John Bogle, Rosabeth Moss Kanter, and W. Edwards Deming. The following is a brief summary of the background and key thoughts on leadership of each. All of their thoughts have a foundation in solid academic research and apply to all levels of leadership *(remember, we are talking about leadership in its broadest sense).*

EFFECTIVE LEADERSHIP BY PETER DRUCKER

Peter Drucker (1909 – 2005) is *"one of the best known and influential thinkers and writers on management theory and practice."* He was an American management consultant and educator, is considered the founder of modern management, and is the author of many books and articles including the leadership classic, *The Effective Executive* (2008).

Drucker has written that effective leader qualities *"are all over the map in terms of their personalities, attitudes, values, strengths and weaknesses. They range from extroverted to nearly reclusive, from easy going to controlling, from generous to parsimonious."* However, late in his career (2004), Drucker once again reaffirmed the eight practices that he believed are the backbone of effective leadership. I believe that Drucker would agree that the attributes apply to anyone that *"impacts others."* They are:

1) **Effective leaders get the knowledge that they need.** They ask others what needs to be done. They simplify and focus on a few, important priorities. They continuously update the cycle of information, focus, and priorities. Effective leaders give *"hands on"* attention to specific tasks in which they are particularly well qualified.

2) **Effective leaders constantly ask:** *Are the plans and actions the right thing for the ongoing success of the enterprise as a whole?* To Drucker, this meant that the enterprise interests must be aligned with all stakeholders *(investors, employees, suppliers, customers, and society in general)*,

or sooner or later there will be an enterprise failure *(and leadership failure)*.

3) **Effective leaders have written action plans.** They know *"knowledge is useless until it has been translated into deeds."* Drucker was the founder of the management by objectives concept which focuses on desired results, actions, and milestones on the way to achieving the results. Effective leader action plans consider all potential obstacles and considerations *(legal, ethical, values, policies, mission)* before implementation.

4) **Effective leaders take responsibility for their decisions and ensure others know their specific accountabilities.** *(The who, what, and by when.)* Effective leaders continuously review decisions and accountabilities and know personnel decisions and personnel development are critical.

5) **Effective leaders take responsibility for communication and a collaborative environment.** They ensure that everyone has the information that they need to get the job done.

6) **Effective leaders ensure problems are solved but focus first on opportunities.** They view technology, market, competitor, product, operations *(etc.)* change as an opportunity for improving results, not a threat. Effective leaders find the best people to develop the opportunities.

7) **Effective leaders spend most of their time meeting with other people.** Communicating, listening, gathering information, and always ensuring that the interchange is issue driven and productive.

8) **Effective leaders think in terms of** *"we,"* **not** *"I."* They think of the needs of the staff and organization before they think of their own.

Leaders according to Drucker: *"listen first, speak last."* And know that...

> *"Management is doing things right,*
> *leadership is getting the right things done."*

INSPIRATIONAL LEADERSHIP BY WARREN BENNIS

Warren Bennis (1929 – 2014) is widely regarded as a *"pioneer of the field of leadership studies"* and has been referred to as the *"dean of leadership gurus."* And through his leadership research efforts over decades he earned the title, *"father of leadership."* He was an educator, organization consultant, and author, writing many books including his best known, *On Becoming a Leader.* His books are well researched and based on interviews with hundreds of leaders from many fields.

Bennis is best known for drawing a contrast between managers and leaders and making the distinction between the command and control management model to a model where authentic leaders create an environment that inspires others to follow. Highlights of Bennis' view of *"inspirational leadership"* *(my term, not his)* are as follows:

- **Inspirational leaders know** *"integrity is the most important characteristic of a leader, and one that he or she must be prepared to demonstrate again and again."* Integrity means words and actions are aligned. They understand that just because something is legal, doesn't mean it is right. They understand that it is all about trust; they build an organization where followers know the leader will do the right thing, has strong values, and will stick to the organization's values. They have a strong moral compass.

- **Inspirational leaders have the capacity to create a compelling vision.** They have a guiding vision and the strength to persist in the face of setbacks. They have the ability to rally others by creating the shared vision, a vision that others are willing to share as their own. They possess the *"Nobel Factor: Optimism, Faith, Hope;"* they communicate optimism to the people around them on the basis that leader optimism is contagious.

- **Inspirational leaders pay attention and know what goes on throughout the organization.** They are attuned to their followers and *"richly endowed with empathy."* They cultivate a culture of candor. They are good listeners and encourage *"backtalk."* They have people in their lives who will tell them the truth, even when it hurts. They encourage dissent and surround themselves with people who have complimentary views. *"No leader becomes truly great unless he or she accepts, even embraces, candor."*

- **Inspirational leaders are curious.** They *"wonder about everything; they want to learn as much as they can."* They are not afraid of making mistakes and admit them when they do. They embrace errors. They create an environment where responsible risk taking is encouraged. They tell people who work for them that the only mistakes are to do nothing and to aim too low. They learn from adversity.

- **Inspirational leaders understand the Pygmalion effect in management.** That is... what managers expect of their subordinates and the way they treat them, largely determines their performance. They set the expectations high *(and realistic),* provide support, and give credit where credit is due. They credit their subordinates with success and accept personal responsibility for failures.

- **Inspirational leaders have the** *"Gretzky Factor."* In other words, they anticipate where the puck is going to be! They have the sense of where the culture is going to be and what the organization needs to do to grow to meet the challenge. They have the ability to have a vision of the future while dealing with the present. They have the ability to *"respond quickly and intelligently to relentless change"* and to *"shape events, rather than being shaped by them."* They *"do not accept things as they are, but rather anticipate things as they can be."*

- **Inspirational leaders value mentors.** Bennis was one of the most sought after business leadership consultants in history. Bennis advised presidents, business leaders, and students, and along the way became one of the most generous of mentors. Bennis believed that great leaders seek out and always have great mentors. They know that mentors will find things in them that they did not know existed and will challenge them to do more than they thought they could.

- **Inspirational leaders** *"understand stakeholder symmetry."* They know they must balance the interest of all stake-holders for the long-term.

- **Inspirational leaders stay the course with constancy of purpose**. They don't ever create surprises for followers. They walk the talk with no gap between what they say and what they do. They reliably spend whatever time and energy necessary to get the job done. They dedicate themselves to the success of the team.

Leaders according to Bennis have...

> *"... the capacity to translate vision into reality."*

AUTHENTIC LEADERSHIP BY BILL GEORGE

Bill George brings knowledge and thoughtfulness regarding leadership as a successful former chairman and CEO of Medtronic, as well as an academic. He now studies and teaches business and leadership at the Harvard Business School. His 2003 book, *Authentic Leadership*, is based on his life's leadership experiences and observations. The book has become a highly respected classic on leadership. George is widely recognized as one of America's premier business leaders and *Authentic Leadership* is one of the most important, insightful leadership books of our time. The following are the clear and insightful messages from the book:

✓ **Authentic leadership is about honesty, devotion to customers, and stewardship of all other stakeholders' interests for the long-term.** Authentic leaders understand that excessive emphasis on shareholder value can be misplaced and shareholder value ultimately only comes from serving customers. They understand that all stakeholders must be served for the overall organization to be successful.

✓ **Authentic leaders have a conviction about ethics.** They have firm values. They *"know they are defined by their values and their character... when their principles are tested, they refuse to compromise."* They believe that values must be constantly reinforced and consistently reflected in the actions of leaders.

✓ **Authentic leaders have a strong sense of purpose.** They know why they do what they do.

✓ **Authentic leaders overcome obstacles.** They are *"able to stand alone against the majority,"* if necessary to do the right thing. They are consistent and self-disciplined. They convert their values into consistent actions. They *"walk the talk."* They are values driven but also performance driven, having a strong commitment to performance standards.

✓ **Authentic leaders build relationships that connect them with others and others with each other.** *"Others follow them because they know where they stand."* They understand that *"it is the openness and the depth of the relationship with the leader that trust and commitment are built."* Authentic leaders understand that collaboration and teams produce the best results.

✓ **Authentic leaders have a balanced life.** Because *"balanced leaders develop healthier people and organizations."* They understand that people who let business dominate their lives expect others to do the same, which is unreasonable and unrealistic.

Leaders according to George have...

"... the ability to ignite the souls of their employees to achieve greatness far beyond what anyone imagined possible."

Steward Leadership by John Bogle

John Bogle (1929 – 2019) is the model for stewardship and leadership. And he is my role model for a lot of reasons.

Bogle, as previously noted, was the contrarian founder of The Vanguard Group of mutual funds. He served as the chief executive of Vanguard from its founding in 1974 until 1999 when he started the Bogle Financial Markets Research Center.

He has written twelve books throughout his life, all with a theme of character, stewardship, corporate values, customer, and community service. He died in 2019 and left behind enormous insight and advice.

In the book, *Enough,* written in 2009, Bogle provides a framework for what I call steward leadership, a term I believe best represents how Bogle viewed leadership. The primary theme of the book is that individuals *(leaders)* have gotten out of balance to the detriment of themselves, the organizations that they lead or represent, and society in general. They are no longer good stewards.

Bogle frames his lessons for *"steward leadership" (my term, not his)* as follows:

⇒ **Steward leaders place stakeholders' interests first.** Any conflict between the *"business"* interests or *"personal"* interests should be resolved in the favor of the interests of all stakeholders.

⇒ **Steward leaders believe in providing meaningful stewardship, trusteeship, and fiduciary responsibility for all actions.** And they do it whether it is legally required or not. They look out for the best interests of all others that their decisions affect.

⇒ **Steward leaders choose simple.** *"When confronted with multiple solutions to a problem, choose the simplest one."* They use common sense and strive for clarity, consistency and predictability, low cost, and innovation that works.

⇒ **Steward leaders add value in everything they do and inspire others to do likewise.** Adding value to all stakeholders is the *"highest priority."* Steward leaders do not *"sell"* the latest fad; they make decisions and investments that add value to stakeholders for the long-term.

⇒ **Steward leaders minimize speculation.** They make decisions that are clearly good for all stakeholders in the long-term.

⇒ **Steward leaders are trustworthy.** In business, data can be used to prove almost anything. Facts, values, and commitments have to hold *"steady as a rock."*

⇒ **Steward leaders are true to the traditional standards of *professional* conduct.** They are committed to the interest of their clients and society in general, they know what they are doing and grow their knowledge, render judgements with integrity, and respect and value oversight.

⇒ **Steward leaders value character over wealth, fame, and power.** *Enough said.*

Bogle sums up his view of leadership by stating: leadership is all about caring for your stakeholders and organization, setting high standards and sticking to them, repeating your values endlessly, understanding that actions speak louder than words, not over managing, recognizing individual achievements, understanding loyalty is a two-way street, leading for the long-term, and being persistent. In two words, leaders are *good stewards.*

True to the title of Bogle's last book, *Stay the Course,* Bogle's leaders *"stay the course"* by always speaking the truth, being fact driven, and looking out for the interests of customers and all other stakeholders.

I, for one, will miss the character-driven, consistent, thoughtful, fearless ways of John Bogle, but look forward to using his legacy and lessons in everything I do. After all *(and again)*...

"What does it all mean if there is no honor and character?"

CHANGE LEADERSHIP BY ROSABETH MOSS KANTER

Rosabeth Moss Kanter is a professor of business at Harvard Business School and the director of the Harvard University Advanced Leadership Initiative. She has written numerous books, particularly on *"strategy, innovation and leadership for change."* Her book, *Change Masters,* has been described as one of the most influential business books of the 20th century. She has received numerous awards recognizing her well-researched contributions to the study of management and social issues. She teaches, writes, and consults with the world's top leaders and is regularly recognized as one of the *"most powerful women"* and *"most influential business thinkers"* in the world.

Kanter once summed up her thoughts on leadership by her *"Six Keys to Leading Positive Change:"*

1) **Show up:** Nothing happens if you don't show up.

2) **Speak up:** Use your voice to shape the agenda and frame and communicate issues. Spread knowledge and share ideas.

3) **Look up:** To a higher principle, vision, and values. Know what you stand for and define the bigger purpose for others to see and follow.

4) **Team up:** Everything goes better with partners.

5) **Never give up:** All ventures hit obstacles. Find a way around the obstacles to reach success.

6) **Lift others up:** Share success, share credit, and give back once you have a success.

The following are other highlights *(sourced in her various books and articles)* of Kanter's thoughts as they relate to change leadership:

❖ Change leaders *"encourage innovation, begin with execution, and name the strategy later."* They place more emphasis on implementation, knowing success or failure depends more on the execution than the strategy.

❖ Change leaders *"question everything."* They keep everyone informed of overall strategy but then empower others to work out implementation details. *"Try, test, learn, modify."*

❖ Change leaders start the *"snowball rolling."* They provide the necessary resources, training, and support and then, let others innovate and execute.

❖ **Change leaders have strong alliances.** They build them within the organization through networking with superiors, peers, and subordinates. Their effectiveness is the result of the ability to influence others.

❖ **Change leaders believe in encouragement and empowerment.** They promote reasonable workloads, empower others to have control of their work, and ensure rewards are commensurate to the contribution.

In the Introduction of Kanter's business classic, *Change Masters*, she writes, effective leaders in an ever-changing world must *"search for ways to involve the entire workforce in innovative problem solving."* She further elaborates by writing that effective leaders facilitate structures, cultures, and reward systems that *"encourage entrepreneurial behavior and employee involvement leading to productive, responsive changes." (Funny, didn't we just talk about having an entrepreneurial spirit?)*

Leaders according to Kanter know...

"If you give up, by definition it's a failure."

... and change leaders never give up.

TOTAL QUALITY LEADERSHIP BY
W. EDWARDS DEMING

W. Edwards Deming (1900 – 1993) is considered the founding father of Total Quality Management (TQM). He and his concepts helped support the turnaround of Japan's post-World War II economy, particularly the automotive and electronics industries. Later, the adoption of Deming's TQM principles helped rejuvenate the manufacturing industry in the United States. Most successful companies use Deming principles in their management today although many call it something else. Some believe TQM is just about the *"quality"* piece, but to me it is more about the *"management" (i.e., leadership)* and Deming had plenty to say on the subject. The following are the timeless, *"total quality"* leader highlights:

❖ Total Quality (TQ) leaders understand that *"the consumer is the most important part of the production line."* All focus is aimed at the needs of the customer. TQ leaders *"transform"* organizations so everyone is responsible for improvement, change, and serving customers.

❖ TQ leaders have *"constancy of purpose"* over the long-term. They eliminate the obsession with short-term thinking and are always looking for ways to improve the business within a strategic vision. They set plans and milestones while remaining consistent with long-term goals and ambitions.

❖ **TQ leaders ensure quality of products and services is built in by proactively controlling processes.** Deming's leaders *"cease dependence on inspection"* and focus on elimination of process variances, root causes of problems, and permanent fixes. They move from fault detection to fault prevention. They correct the process and train the people.

❖ **TQ leaders provide more and better training of employees.** They ensure a wider array of skills is attained and give employees more flexibility and responsibility to do their jobs. They help employees grow and ensure they are provided with the proper tools and training to do their jobs more effectively.

❖ **TQ leaders promote collaboration and eliminate barriers between functions.** They promote the concept of internal as well as external customers, and the one common goal – meeting all customer needs. They do not manage by fear of failure. They encourage innovation, transparency, open communication, and new ideas. They drive for quality, not quantity, knowing that improved quality will lead to increased productivity *(Deming and others have proved it time and again)*.

❖ **TQ leaders have continuous improvement as a philosophy *(improve constantly and forever)*.** They strive to create an environment where all employees look for ways to improve products and services to meet customer needs.

Late in his life, Deming was once asked how he would like to be remembered. He said:

> *"If at all... as someone who spent his life trying to keep America from committing suicide."*

The comment seems prophetic to me. Ineffective leaders all over the place who have not followed the *"roads"* paved by Drucker, Bennis, George, Bogle, Kanter, and Deming have destroyed *(or at least damaged)* their organizations to the detriment of themselves and their stakeholders.

There is plenty of good advice on leadership choices offered by these leadership greats. Although there are several common themes, each offers a slightly different perspective for a leader who is effective, inspirational, and authentic, and is a good steward who drives change and promotes total quality in the broadest sense. And I believe all combined are key ingredients of successful leaders.

MY MILE MARKERS ON THE ROAD
TO GENUINE LEADERSHIP

My perspective of leadership is derived from thoughtful observations during my academic education and professional education, as well as my time as a Big Four auditor, a director of an Internal Audit function, a professor of higher education, and as an entrepreneur.

But more importantly, it is derived from both my genuine experiences of being led and of leading others. It came from working for someone I learned nothing from and working for someone I learned many things from. It came from working for myself. It came from real-life, in the trenches, learning from mistakes, celebrating what works leadership practice. It came from taking the time to build a leadership philosophy, communicating that philosophy, and genuinely living and leading by that philosophy *every* day.

I will try not to overlap too much with the experts and role models; however, the following are my collective suggestions for what I call *"genuine leadership."* See Exhibit VI in the Appendix for *The Genuine Leader Scale* to measure yourself.

√ **A genuine leader is a model for ethical behavior and inspires others to do likewise.** They know that individuals tend to act the way they talk, so they talk about ethics and act accordingly. They know that one *"white lie"* can send a signal that hypocrisy is okay and open the floodgates for lying, falsification, and misrepresentation. They are an *everyday ethicist.*

√ **A genuine leader is never a *"lapdog."*** The term may be offensive – if so, I apologize. However, almost every scandal that I read about has a *"lapdog leader,"* or maybe even an entire *"lapdog department."* The CFO at Enron was one. Bernie Madoff had one. Genuine leaders know they have an ethical responsibility to their shareholders, customers, regulators, employees, and communities, *first.* You *may* be tested in big ways; you *will* be tested in many small ways. Be prepared to report ethical and policy violations *(by anyone)* to whoever it takes to get the message out, and if necessary, resign. Your reputation is more important than a job.

√ **A genuine leader loves their whistleblowers.** They provide safe mechanisms for employees to report ethics, conduct, values, and policy violations. They foster open communications between leadership and all stakeholders without fear of retaliation. They listen to everything, even the things that aren't fun to hear. They have more than an open-door policy, they have a *no-door* policy. They are prepared to sort through all the non-serious issues to find the one issue that is really critical to the future of the business and organization.

√ **A genuine leader never lets a crisis go to waste.** They let every crisis develop their character and the character of their employees and their organization. When a crisis occurs *(ethical, financial, operational, etc.)* they take timely, definitive action and communicate to all in the organization to reinforce the seriousness. Heightened awareness is a learning opportunity.

√ **A genuine leader knows professional conduct trumps business conduct.** In the basic sense, business standards of behavior are simply to make money and not break the law. A genuine leader doesn't believe this is good enough. They apply a professional conduct framework of respect and integrity for *all* stakeholder interests. Remember what I said previously on the road of the everyday ethicist, *"any conflicts between professional (ethical) conduct and business conduct must be reconciled in favor of the stakeholders (professional conduct)."* The customer and integrity come first.

√ **A genuine leader doesn't overcommit or exaggerate.** *It is much better that the truth beats what you say than if what you say falls short of the truth.* They are fact driven based on observations, data, logic, analysis, and reason, and are objective and impartial. They are not swayed into making bad decisions based on relationships and financial incentives. They are aware of potential exaggerations and embellishments. They ensure they accurately commit and deliver on their commitments, and they teach others to do the same. *They believe a promise is a promise.*

√ **A genuine leader provides a moderating influence and a reality check on unrealistic goals and objectives.** They do not perpetuate the lie of an unrealistic goal that often results in cutting corners, short cuts, compromises, and fudging the results. They are prepared to focus resources on process, quality, and checks and balances.

√ **A genuine leader delivers their function by listening to the needs of employees.** They meet one-on-one, they walk around, they hold skip level meetings, and they utilize surveys and obtain feedback however possible to find out what is *really* going on at their organization. They are transparent in knowledge and actions. They are vulnerable and admit mistakes. They develop meaningful personal and professional relationships. They mentor others.

The last genuine leadership quality I will mention can sometimes be the most difficult. There are many obstacles we face as leaders – bumps in the road *(or those potholes again)*, mountains to climb – but in order to inspire our onlookers we have to *stay steady* no matter the road conditions. Be constant, be consistent... *stay steady on the ride.*

THIS IS THE GENUINE LEADERSHIP CHOICE.

"Somebody has to take responsibility for being a leader."
– Toni Morrison

MY FAVORITE LEADERSHIP QUOTES

"I've learned that people will forget what you said,
people will forget what you did,
but people will never forget how you made them feel."
– Maya Angelou

"Management is doing things right;
leadership is doing the right things."
– Peter Drucker

"Successful leaders see the opportunities in every difficulty
rather than the difficulty in every opportunity."
– Reed Markham

"A leader is one who knows the way, goes the way,
and shows the way."
– John C. Maxwell

"Leadership is about making others better as a result
of your presence and making sure that impact lasts in
your absence."
– Sheryl Sandberg

"Great groups need to know that the person at the top will fight
like a tiger for them."
– Warren Bennis

"If you want to go fast, go alone.
If you want to go far, go together."
– Bill George

"The transformation will come from leadership."
– W. Edwards Deming

EXPLORE YOUR GENUINE LEADERSHIP CHOICES.

What are your qualities that influence others to want to follow your lead?

What are your qualities that have driven others away?

Do others trust you? Why or why not?

How do you make others feel?

Are you transparent? How do you show others that you "walk the talk?"

How do you make others feel during a crisis? How are your crisis management skills?

Do you admit mistakes?

How would you describe your problem-solving skills?

In what ways do you help others to become more effective? What could you do to help more?

Do you have a mentor? Are you a mentor?

How are you at communicating? Listening?

Are you constant and steadfast (or sporadic and unpredictable)?

What is your genuine leadership philosophy going to be? What is your plan to communicate your philosophy?

CHOOSING HABITS:

THE POWER OF IDENTITY

"I have learned that champions aren't just born; champions can be made when they embrace and commit to life-changing positive habits."
– Lewis Howes

CHOOSE YOUR PATH WISELY

A HABIT IS DEFINED AS *"a settled or regular tendency or practice, especially one that is hard to give up."* It is a routine behavior done on a regular basis. A habit is a behavior that, when done once felt so good, now is done without thinking. The repetition automates the behavior and turns it into a habit.

In his book, *The Power of Habit*, Charles Duhigg summarizes a lot of research on how habits are formed and how they function. Duhigg points out those habits are comprised of three parts: an environmental cue, a behavioral response, and a reward *(e.g., social situation, several glasses of wine, nice little buzz).*

Unfortunately, the *"cues"* have no conscience – the cue may trigger good behavior, or it may trigger bad behavior. That's the dilemma. Sometimes habits can be random, unpredictable, and unproductive.

Do you want to live a random, unpredictable, and unproductive life? Do you want to be *"identified"* as someone who is random, unpredictable, and unproductive? I would call this life by accident or happenstance. A life driven by habits – good and bad. A life with no plan.

When discussing *"habits"* many point out that we are the sum of our daily habits, *"small efforts,"* and routines. Often quoted people remind us that:

> *"We become what we repeatedly do."*
> – Sean Covey
>
> *"We are what we repeatedly do."*
> – Will Durant
>
> *"...our habits make us."*
> – John Dryden

Truth is, they are probably correct... but is this enough for *you?* What is the rest of *your* story? What is *your* identity? Who do *you really* want to be? If we are the sum of our daily habits, do your daily habits and activities support your desired identity?

A person who first "chooses" an identity can develop the habits that support that identity.

THE PSYCHOLOGISTS' RIDDLES – ANSWERED

> *Are bad habits the cause of alcoholism*
> *or the result of alcoholism?*
> *Are good habits the result of good health*

> *or the cause of good health?*
> *Is alcoholism the result of bad habits*
> *or the cause of bad habits?*
> *Is a healthy lifestyle the result of good habits*
> *or the cause of good habits?*

You get the point. Most would say it is a vicious cycle, a *"catch 22."* Mutually conflicting conditions. The practical answer is that it is a little of both.

However, to me, it is not a riddle. The choice is clear. **Be proactive.** Choose your identity and choose the characteristics that define your identity. Then, build your habits to support what you want to be. If you choose to live a healthy lifestyle, choose habits that support that lifestyle. If you choose to be more organized, choose habits that support that goal.

For example, it should be obvious from the contents of this book that I want you to be someone who embraces and grows from adversity. I want you to treasure learning new things and to be a person of great character. I want you to have an owner's mindset and an entrepreneurial spirit. And I want you to be a genuine leader. *So how can you accomplish this?*

Define this as your *"optimum identity."* Then, build your daily routine, your focus, around supporting this identity. Determine the regular and repeated habits that you will make your own to ensure your desired optimum identity becomes a reality.

So, here are all the hard questions. Are your habits consistent with your values and your long-term plans? Do your habits help or hinder you in the achievement of your goals? Do your habits match your identity... who you are and what you want to be? If your habits aren't a match and are not helping, you have a choice: You can either wait for a crisis, or you can *be proactive* and change. You can ditch your bad habits and choose good ones... ones that support your optimum identity. *Easy, right?* Unfortunately, we all know, *it isn't that easy.* So, let's discuss where to start.

HOW TO IMPROVE YOUR HABITS

As Amy Johnson writes in her book, *The Little Book of Big Change:*

> *"You are not a fixed entity with fixed habits –*
> *you are fresh in each moment,*
> *with infinite possibilities available to you."*

The wisdom to choose your identity is within each of us. We have introduced many *"choices"* in the previous chapters – choices that we have when we are facing *adversity*, seeking *self-development*, determining our *character*, taking *ownership* in our lives, and when we are *leading*. In all cases, as we thoughtfully conduct a self-assessment of ourselves and our choices *(which is the primary goal of this book)*, the question becomes, how can we *be sure* that we will change our behavior in order to capitalize on the opportunities that we have identified.

What do we do to ensure that we have the appropriate "habits" to live our values and achieve our goals?

The experts seem to offer a couple options. One is to make a list of *"what"* you want to change/improve and go to work on them. I think that's an okay choice, in fact, we have an exercise for identifying good habits and bad ones in the accompanying *Choices* workbook.

Another option, however, centers on *"who"* you want to become. This approach is recommended by habit expert, James Clear, in his book, *Atomic Habits.* His recommended approach leads to a creation of *"identity-based habits."*

Through the identity-based approach, to change a habit first requires the person to identify the underlying beliefs that created it. In other words, reinvent yourself and what you want to be. To change habits in a lasting way requires a realignment of behaviors to match the desired *identity.*

He offers the example of people who decide to take pride in their athletic skills. They will carry out the habits affiliated with maintaining their physical ability and their identity as athletes. The *"athlete"* is likely to adopt a daily routine that puts the self-image into action. The individual will have a regular routine of workouts or sporting activities, as the process of honing and improving athletic ability calls for continuous, repetitive activity *(i.e., habits).*

Let's go through some more identity examples. **I would think an identity of being *"healthy"* would be a good ambition.** When we think of a healthy lifestyle, we might expect habits such as:

- ✓ A healthy diet with regular intake of healthy foods like vegetables, fruits, nuts, whole grains, healthy fats, etc.

- ✓ A healthy level of physical activity that might be the typically recommended 30 minutes a day *(of walking, running, swimming, biking, Pilates, CrossFit, yoga, etc. – so many choices).*

- ✓ A low intake of alcohol, not using tobacco products of any kind, and maintaining a healthy body weight *(BMI).*

How about an identity of healthy mental state? We might expect habits such as:

- ✓ Daily practice of focusing your attention *(e.g., mindful meditation).*

- ✓ Getting consistently good rest with the same sleep routines daily.

- ✓ Re-enforcing boundaries regarding your values by daily stating them and living them.

- ✓ Organizing your workspace to minimize distractions.

- ✓ Routinely focusing on the positive.

How about an identity of being highly productive? We would expect habits such as:

- ✓ Developing stretch goals that promote new ways of thinking.

- ✓ Routinely setting schedules and creating action plans.

- ✓ Monitoring timelines to identify whether goals are being met efficiently.

- ✓ Regularly asking for feedback from people you trust.

How about an identity of initiative and follow through? We would expect habits such as:

- ✓ Setting our own goals and self-monitoring progress.

- ✓ Meeting commitments on time, every time.

- ✓ Being motivated to learn what is needed to complete work.

- ✓ Really believing and practicing *"a promise is a promise."*

How about an identity of doing high-quality work? We would expect habits such as:

- ✓ Paying regular attention to detail.
- ✓ Consistently performing accurate work.
- ✓ Ensuring clear quality standards.
- ✓ Establishing consistent processes.

How about an identity as a good problem solver? We would expect habits such as:

- ✓ Clearly framing the problem to be solved.
- ✓ Practicing skills using the latest problem-solving tools.
- ✓ Making fact-based decisions.
- ✓ Keeping an open mind.
- ✓ Believing in and looking for simple solutions.
- ✓ Being persistent.

How about an identity as a team player? We would expect habits such as:

- ✓ Being a regular listener *(not a habitual interrupter)*.
- ✓ Consistently working well with others.
- ✓ Proactively helping others.
- ✓ Raising the level of work of others.

How about an identity as someone with good organization skills? We would expect habits such as:

- ✓ Keeping your workspace and work files well organized *(seriously, your workspace says a lot about your identity)*.

✓ Ensuring your email inbox is manageable *(and using other electronic means of organization, i.e., folders).*

✓ Keeping a daily *"to-do"* list for today's activities and perhaps tomorrow's to dos.

✓ Maintaining a system of prioritizing activities to *"major on the majors."*

✓ Having a procedure for tracking project status.

How about an identity of someone who is punctual with good time management skills? We would expect habits such as:

✓ Regular routines to start your day.

✓ Showing up on time, every time for meetings and engagements.

✓ Executing your daily schedule with short interval planning and necessary reminders.

✓ Combining like work to improve focus and efficiency while allowing for flexibility.

Note: The above examples just happen to be habits that are often cited as the habits of highly effective and productive people and *"President's Award"* recipients.

OUR CHOICES, OUR IDENTITY, OUR HABITS

Again, in previous chapters, we have discussed our *choices* for embracing adversity, nurturing development, building character, creating ownership, and providing genuine leadership. So now that we know that this could be our *optimum identity,* let's discuss what *habits* we would expect for each:

Embracing Adversity

⇒ Understanding adversity cannot be anticipated and embracing it when it happens.

⇒ Reaching out for support.

⇒ Becoming more self-aware and forward thinking.

⇒ Taking action, changing, and growing from adversity.

Nurturing Development

⇒ Engaging in self-assessment and self-awareness exercises.

⇒ Finding your passion and setting your goals.

⇒ Being gritty and persistent in tasks.

⇒ Earning respect by problem solving.

Building Character

⇒ Recognizing unethical behavior vulnerabilities.

⇒ Developing your own values and ethical standards.

⇒ Living your values.

⇒ Being a model for ethical conduct for others.

⇒ Choosing character over your job, money, or relationships *(wealth, power, or fame)*.

Creating Ownership

⇒ Exceeding commitments.

⇒ Engaging customers at every opportunity.

⇒ Solving problems for customers.

⇒ Paying it forward, continuously.

Providing Genuine Leadership

⇒ Maintaining high moral, ethical, professional, and personal standards for self and others.

⇒ Being transparent, vulnerable, and admitting and accepting mistakes.

⇒ Listening and serving the balanced interests of others.

⇒ Maintaining a healthy work/life balance and enabling others to do so.

See Exhibit VII in the Appendix for my *Optimum Identities for Strivers and Thrivers.* Print it, post it, add to it as you see fit... to live your optimum identity.

HOW TO GET RID OF BAD HABITS?

> *"A bad habit never disappears miraculously;*
> *It's an undo-it-yourself project."*
> – Abigail Van Buren

Experts seem to agree that it is difficult to change your habits. Heck, I didn't need an expert to tell me that, and I'm sure you didn't either.

But the wisdom required to get rid of your bad habits is already in your mind. Amy Johnson points out human beings have free will and *"free won't"* – the ability to not act. Questionable habits should be approached much like ethical decisions:

• Recognize everyone has bad habits.

• Understand that breaking bad habits is hard work.

- Make sure your bad habits do not harm others.

- Pause before acting and notice the *"choice point."*

- Commit to a pre-set game plan for handling certain *"cue"* situations.

- Get counsel from others.

- Judge your own bad habits the way you would judge others.

- Visualize your habits displayed on the front page of the paper, in front of a judge, your mother, or your child.

- Let every *"bad habit crisis"* strengthen your resolve to improve.

James Clear *(Atomic Habits)* reminds us that every bad habit is initiated by a *"cue."* To eliminate the bad habit, remove the cue that triggered it. Change the routine. He says, *"it is easier to avoid the temptation than resist it."* Watch who you hang out with and where you go.

When overwhelmed by a large problem or a big goal, we break it down into small steps. The same thing applies to habits. Don't start with a marathon; walk around the block first. Engage in activities that match your ability. But remember to log your progress to recognize how far you have come. Stephen Guise in his book, *Mini Habits*, points out that a mini habit is *"too small to fail"* because it takes little will power and quickly results in success. *Under commit and over deliver when it comes to habit changing.*

There is much advice out there regarding changing habits. They fall in several camps. One says it is best to build and strengthen your good habits. Another says, focus on your bad habits and correct, modify, or eliminate. Yet another piece of advice says, *replace* your bad habits with good ones.

But I believe the best way to get rid of bad habits is to simply join the *"Identity Protection Program."*

Rule Number 1: Choose your identity and fill up your life with habits that support what you want to be.

Rule Number 2: Choose your identity and fill up your life with habits that support what you want to be.

Rule Number 3: Choose your identity and fill up your life with habits that support what you want to be.

Choose your identity path wisely. You don't need to *pretend* your life depends on it because *it does. We are the sum of ALL our choices.*

THIS IS THE IDENTITY AND HABITS CHOICE.

*"There are three constants in life –
change, choice, and principles."*
– Steven Covey

MY FAVORITE HABIT QUOTES

*"You'll never change your life until you change something you
do daily. The secret of your success is found in your daily
routine."*
– John C. Maxwell

*"I learned that if I am going to enjoy the here and now, I need
to relieve myself of the things that slow me down."*
– Ann Richards

*"We are what we repeatedly do.
Excellence, then, is not an act but a habit."*
– Will Durant

"We first make our habits, and then our habits make us."
– John Dryden

*"Success is the sum of small efforts repeated
day in and day out."*
– Robert Collier

*"Depending on what they are, our habits will either make us or
break us. We become what we repeatedly do."*
– Sean Covey

"It is easier to prevent bad habits than to break them."
– Benjamin Franklin

"Good habits are worth being fanatical about."
– John Irving

"Winning is a habit. Unfortunately, so is losing."
– Vince Lombardi

"The best way to stop a bad habit is to never begin it."
– J.C. Penney

EXPLORE YOUR IDENTITIES AND HABITS CHOICES.

What are your most important identities?

What is your optimum identity?

What good habits will you adopt to bolster your optimum identity?

What good habits will you adopt to enable you to embrace **adversity?**

What good habits will you adopt to **develop yourself?**

What good habits will you adopt to enable you to build your **character?**

What good habits will you adopt to engage your **entrepreneurial spirit?**

What good habits will you adopt to become a **genuine leader?**

What is going to be put on your "not-to-do" list (bad habits) that doesn't support your optimum identity?

Author's Concluding Comments

> "If you don't go after what you want, you'll never have it.
> If you don't ask, the answer is always no.
> If you don't step forward, you're always in the same place."
> – Nora Roberts

IN THE INTRODUCTION of the book, I told you that we all already make choices on this road called life. We make choices in our personal lives. We make choices in our professional lives. We make choices when encountering adversity. We make choices that reflect our character. We make choices that echo our feelings, attitude, motivation, and perspective. We make choices that form our identity and habits, both good and bad. We make choices that shape our careers. We make choices about how we lead. We make choices that turn out to be mistakes. We make choices that turn out to be perfect, life-altering decisions.

We are the sum of our choices.
*The **choices** you make, from this day forward, will determine your **future**.*

If you continued reading *(and I'm hoping you didn't just skip the conclusion),* I hope you can now see the power of making better choices: embracing your adversity and using it to your advantage, developing and implementing an ongoing self-development plan to do more, better, forever aiming for impeccable character, improving your success through an owner mindset and entrepreneurial spirit, leading in a genuine way in everything you do, and establishing a clear identity with supporting, productive habits.

I have presented throughout this book the *"lessons"* from distinguished experts in their respective fields. Hopefully their advice will help you on your road.

I hope I have inspired you with some quotes here and there that got you thinking – *"I can do that"* or *"I never thought of that"* or, better yet, *"I will do that."*

And most importantly, my hope is the questions at the end of each chapter provide a stimulus to discover your authentic self *(as Bill George would say)* and develop a plan full of better choices for your personal and professional life.

Now is the time to implement the plan. There has never been a better time.

⇒ *Are you choosing to grow from your adversities and challenges?*

⇒ *Are you choosing to constantly assess your development needs and put forth the effort to reach your goals?*

⇒ *Are you choosing to become an everyday ethicist, willing to quit your job before you quit your ethics?*

⇒ *Are you choosing to develop and apply your owner's mindset and entrepreneurial spirit?*

⇒ *Are you choosing to be a genuine leader?*

⇒ *Are you choosing your optimum identity and building good habits to support it?*

Be proud of your **choices**. Be courageous in **choosing** to honor your values and achieve your goals.

THIS IS YOUR ROAD. THESE ARE YOUR CHOICES.

I wish you a meaningful, full life and a rewarding career filled with **great choices**.

> *"Life is a matter of choices, and every choice you make makes you."*
> – John C. Maxwell

APPENDIX

EXHIBIT I

THE EMBRACING ADVERSITY GROWTH PLAN (EAGP)

Recognize life is unpredictable and sometimes uncontrollable.

Accept it for what it is and begin to deal with it.

Reach out for support from family, friends, mental health professionals, trusted advisors and counselors.

Conduct an internal self-assessment. Become more self-aware.

Prepare to act.

Initiate a fresh start on your own terms. Move on.

Don't look back.

Escape the past and commit to present and future.

Re-focus part of efforts on helping others dealing with adversity.

Put energy on the door that is opening.

Change, continuously learn, adapt.

Believe in self-development.

"Wake up smarter every day."

EXHIBIT II

SELF-ASSESSMENT QUESTIONS

To be used for self-rating and rating by others.

How do I deal with constructive criticism?

How self-confident am I?

How aware am I of my moods and emotions?

How sensitive am I to the feelings and perspective of others?

How aware am I of the impact I have on other people?

How comfortable am I in dealing with ambiguity and change?

What are my ethical blind spots?

What are my strengths?

What are my weaknesses?

Do my skills and ability match my chosen career path/objectives?

Does my skill and ability enable me to perform my job well?

How are my communications skills?

Do my communication skills match my career level goal?

Am I innovative and creative?

Am I a good listener?

Do I keep my commitments?

Am I a good collaborator and team player?

Am I considered an effective leader?

Am I considered professional?

Do I have good time and project management skills?

Am I genuine and authentic?

EXHIBIT III

THE RESPECT SCALE

Rate yourself on a scale of 1 (least like you) to 5 (most like you).

- Others seek your advice, counsel, and contribution.

- You are assigned or volunteer for projects that no one wants or can do.

- You are known to *"deliver your function"* by setting and meeting goals.

- You have a deep understanding of the organization's mission, values, and objectives.

- You need little direction in effectively supporting organization objectives.

- You fully understand and meet your internal and external customers' needs.

- You have knowledge of best functional, business, and industry practices.

- You learn continuously.

- You *"major on the major"* and don't nit-pick.

- You focus on high return projects and issues.

- You permanently fix the high risk/reward problems.

- You don't waste time and resources.

- You apply the latest tools and techniques of your function.

- You constantly look for ways to be more productive and help others do likewise.

- You embrace change and offer suggestions for improvement.

- Your work is systematic, thorough, complete, and accurate.

- You are personable and approachable.

- You communicate well and listen often.

EXHIBIT IV

THE EVERYDAY ETHICIST CONTRACT

√ Recognize everyone is vulnerable to unethical behavior.

√ Understand that ethical behavior is hard work.

√ Develop your own personal value statement and ethical code of conduct.

√ Do no harm to others.

√ Judge your own ethical decisions the way you would judge others.

√ Visualize defending your actions in front of a judge.

√ Imagine an article on the front page of the Wall Street Journal describing your actions.

√ Project ethical challenges into future situations and pre-commit to intended ethical choices.

√ Practice writing down thoughts to get a clear, developed plan for conduct and actions.

√ Review critical ethical decisions and alternative actions with personal mentors or professional colleagues and/or trusted advisors before acting.

√ Make decisions as if you had trusteeship, stewardship, or fiduciary responsibility for others.

√ Meet or exceed your commitments and do not overcommit or exaggerate.

√ Commit to serve the best interests of clients, in particular, and society, in general.

√ Resolve any conflicts between business interests and personal interests in the favor of others.

√ Let every ethical crisis develop your character and strengthen your resolve to do the right thing.

√ Don't compromise your integrity at any cost.

√ Be a model for ethical conduct; *walk the talk*.

√ Speak up to power.

√ Speak truth to power.

EXHIBIT V

14 TIPS FOR SUCCESSFUL "OWNERS" OF THEIR LIFE

1. Be self-aware and pursue your passion. *All roads start here.*

2. Plan the basics, and then be a doer. *Get moving and be prepared for hard work.*

3. Selling equals trust and trust equals selling. *Always do the right thing.*

4. Engage your customers. *Listen.* Judge your performance by whether customers seek you out.

5. Pay the price of entrepreneurship. Market yourself by giving things away. Go above and beyond. *Sell yourself.*

6. Add value by solving problems. *Make your work matter.* Be prepared to respond to the unforeseen.

7. Be the expert, then be innovative and *unique.*

8. Design and presentation make a difference. *Attractiveness counts.* For you AND your product/service.

9. Build good relationships because they are important to *you.*

10. Be thoroughly professional. Integrity and customers come *first.*

11. Collaborate with quality. Your associates are your brand. *Be someone everyone wants to work with.*

12. Ensure the economics makes sense. Business is business. *But simple can win.*

13. Understand the difference between price and value. *Value drives price.*

14. Pay it forward. *Always.*

EXHIBIT VI

THE GENUINE LEADER SCALE

Rate yourself on a scale of 1 (least like you) to 5 (most like you).

- You maintain high ethics and integrity *(professional and personal)* standards for yourself and others.

- You establish clear values and principles. You have a leadership philosophy.

- You walk the talk.

- You ensure you have the knowledge you need to get the job done.

- You create a compelling vision for others.

- You are transparent.

- You value innovation, continuous improvement, problem solving, and simplicity.

- You have written plans *(goals)* and clear priorities for both short and long term.

- You don't exaggerate.

- You understand product and service quality are derived from controlled processes.

- You live by stewardship, trusteeship, and fiduciary standards.

- You value checks and balances and good governance.

- You serve others' interests and needs first. And you balance interests of all stakeholders.

- You are vulnerable. You take personal responsibility for decisions and failures.

- You are accountable and deliver on your commitments.

- You are observant and know what is going on around you.

- You listen first.

- You are open and honest at all times. But you communicate to all with the upmost respect.

- You promote good relationships; collaboration gets the best results.

- You value your mentors. And you spend time to mentor others.

- You embrace adversity and learn and grow from it.

- You maintain a healthy work/life balance and encourage others to do so.

- You support others with training and opportunity for growth.

- You celebrate and reward others' successes.

- You inspire others to do things they never thought possible.

- You are steadfast and constant.

- You stay the course.

EXHIBIT VII

OPTIMUM IDENTITIES FOR STRIVERS AND THRIVERS

- Embraces and grows from adversity and challenges.

- Knows their passion, sets goals, improves, and persists.

- Exhibits impeccable character; is an everyday ethicist.

- Has an owner mindset and entrepreneurial spirit.

- Is a *genuine* leader. Ethical, effective, authentic, inspirational, total quality, with stewardship for all.

- Works hard on habits that support their identity *(or identities)* of choice, plus other effective habits for:

    o Having a healthy lifestyle and mental state.

    o Being highly productive.

    o Taking initiative and following through.

    o Producing high quality work.

    o Being a problem solver.

    o Being a team player.

    o Staying well organized.

    o Executing commitments timely.

YOUR ROAD. YOUR CHOICES. WORKBOOK CONTENTS

The following is a list of material contained in the *Choices Workbook* available under separate cover.

INTRODUCTION

My Choices, My Road Overview

Explore your Choices from the Past Exercise

CHOOSING TO EMBRACE ADVERSITY

The Art of the Struggle Overview

Explore your Adversity Choices Exercise

Living and Leading in a Crisis: Case Studies and Lessons

CHOOSING DEVELOPMENT

Personal and Professional Effectiveness Overview

The Grit Checklist

The Respect Scale

Tips for Lean Thinking and Solutions

Value Stream Mapping

Job or Project Development Form

Effects Analysis Form

Explore your Development Choices Exercise

CHOOSING IMPECCABLE CHARACTER

Becoming The Everyday Ethicist Overview

The Everyday Ethicist Contract

Checklist for Ethical Decision Making

Character Case Studies

Explore your Character Choices Exercise

SUGGESTED READINGS

THE FOLLOWING are books referenced throughout this book. Others relate to the subject material that I believe provide useful information and messages. *Unbroken* (Hillenbrand) is included because it is the classic tale of adversity. It is the true story of WWII prisoner of war, Louis Zamperini, and his quest for *"survival, resilience, and redemption."* If you have not read the book, read it and grow.

ADVERSITY AND CHALLENGE

George, Bill. (2009). *Seven Lesson for Leading in Crisis.* San Francisco, CA. Jossey-Bass.

Grant, Adam & Sandberg, Sheryl. (2017). *Option B.* New York, NY. Knopf Doubleday Publishing.

Hillenbrand, Laura. (2010). *Unbroken.* New York, NY. Random House Publishing.

Holiday, Ryan. (2014). *The Obstacle Is the Way.* London. Profile Books.

Snyder, Steven. (2013). *Leadership and the Art of Struggle.* Oakland, CA. Berrett-Koehler Publishers.

DEVELOPMENT AND EFFECTIVENESS

Carnegie, Dale. (1936). *How to Win Friends and Influence People.* New York, NY. Pocket Books.

Covey, Stephen R. (1989). *The Seven Habits of Highly Effective People.* New York, NY. Simon and Schuster.

Duckworth, Angela. (2016). *GRIT: The Power of Passion and Perseverance.* New York, NY. Scribner.

Duhigg, Charles. (2016). *Smarter Faster Better.* New York, NY. Random House.

George, Bill. (2015). *Discover Your True North.* Hoboken, NJ. John Wiley & Sons, Inc.

George, B., Craig, N., & Snook, S. (2015). *The Discover Your True North Fieldbook.* Hoboken, NJ. John Wiley & Sons, Inc.

Gladwell, Malcolm. (2000). *The Tipping Point.* Boston, MA. Little, Brown & Co.

Gladwell, Malcolm. (2008). *Outliers.* Boston, MA. Little, Brown & Co.

Peale, Norman Vincent. (1952). *The Power of Positive Thinking.* New York, NY. Touchstone Publishing.

Peters, Tom. (2018). *The Excellence Dividend.* New York, NY. Vintage Books.

Robbins, Anthony. (1986). *Unlimited Power.* New York, NY. Free Press.

Sandberg, Sheryl. (2013). *Lean In.* New York, NY. Knopf Doubleday Publishing.

CHARACTER AND ETHICS

Bazerman, M. H., & Tenbrunsel, A. E. (2012). *Blind Spots.* Princeton, NJ. Princeton University Press.

Bogle, John C. (2009). *Enough.* Hoboken, NJ. John Wiley & Sons, Inc.

Brooks, David. (2015). *The Road to Character.* New York, NY. Random House.

Covey, Stephen M.R. & Merrill, Rebecca R. (2006). *The Speed of Trust.* New York, NY. Free Press.

Fountain, Lynn. (2016). *Ethics and the Internal Auditor's Political Dilemma.* Boca Raton, FL. CRC Press.

Messick, D. M. & Tenbrunsel, A. E. (1996). *Codes of Conduct* New York, NY. Russel Sage Foundation.

OWNERSHIP AND ENTREPRENEURSHIP

Brown, Paul B. (2015). *Entrepreneurship for the Rest of Us.* Brookline, MA. Bibliomotion, Inc.

Brussee, Warren. (2010). *Six Sigma on a Budget.* New York, NY. McGraw Hill Education.

Cathy, S. Truett. (2002). *Doing Business the Chick-fil-A Way.* Decatur, GA. Looking Glass Books.

Fellers, Gary (1994). *Why Things Go Wrong.* Gretna, LA. Pelican Publishing Company.

Hill, Napoleon. (1937). *Think and Grow Rich.* New York, NY. Random House Publishing.

Hopkins, Mark (2013). 10 Entrepreneurial Habits and a Roadmap for an Exceptional Career. Austin, TX. Greenleaf Book Group.

Kawasaki, Guy (2019). *Wise Guy*. New York, NY. Penguin Random House.

Peters, T. & Waterman, R. (1982) *In Search of Excellence*. New York, NY. Collins Business Essentials.

Peters, Tom. (1999). *The Professional Service Firm 50*. New York, NY. Knopf Publishing.

Womack, J. P. & Jones, D. T. (2005). *Lean Solutions*. New York, NY. Simon & Schuster.

GENUINE LEADERSHIP

Bennis, Warren. (2009). *On Becoming a Leader*. Philadelphia, PA. Basic Books.

Bogle, John C. (2009). *Enough*. Hoboken, NJ. John Wiley & Sons, Inc.

Bogle, John C. (2019). *Stay the Course*. Hoboken, NJ. John Wiley & Sons, Inc.

Collins, James C. (2001). *Good to Great*. New York, NY. William Collins.

Dalio, Ray. (2017). *Principles of Life and Work*. New York, NY. Simon & Schuster.

Deming, W. Edwards. (1994). *The New Economics*. Cambridge, MA. The MIT Press.

Deming, W. Edwards. (1982). *Out of the Crisis*. Cambridge, MA. The MIT Press.

Drucker, Peter. (1967). *The Effective Executive.* New York, NY. Harper Business Essentials.

George, William. (2003). *Authentic Leadership.* San Francisco, CA. Josey-Bass.

Isaacson, Walter. (2011). *Steve Jobs.* New York, NY. Simon & Schuster.

Kanter, Rosabeth Moss. (1983). *Change Masters.* New York, NY. Simon & Schuster.

IDENTITY AND HABITS

Burchard, Brendon. (2017). High Performance Habits. Carlsbad, CA. Hay House Publishing.

Clear, James. (2018). Atomic Habits. New York, NY. Avery Publishing.

Covey, Stephen R. & Hatch, David K. (2006). Everyday Greatness. Nashville, TN. Thomas Nelson Publishing.

Dunhigg, Charles. (2012). The Power of Habit. New York, NY. Random House.

Fiore, Neil. (2007). The Now Habit. New York, NY. Penguin Random House.

Guise, Stephen. (2013). Mini Habits. Scotts Valley, CA. CreateSpace Publishing.

Johnson, Amy (2016). The Little Book of Big Change. Oakland, CA. New Harbinger Publishing.

ABOUT THE AUTHOR

AMANDA "JO" ERVEN , CPA, CIA, CFE

Internal Audit Strategist

Management Consultant

Continuing Professional Education Trainer

Higher Education Professor

Keynote Speaker

Author

Amanda "Jo" is the President and Founder of Audit. Consulting. Education. LLC, a firm specializing in progressive Internal Auditing and management consulting and providing impactful CPE hours to organizations and individuals, globally.

Jo is a Certified Public Accountant (CPA), a Certified Internal Auditor (CIA), and a Certified Fraud Examiner (CFE) who pushes the envelope of traditional Internal Auditing. She believes audit should no longer be *"reactive"* and should focus on *"proactive,"* real value-add activities, melding quality and ethical behavior into the organization. Her trademarked approach to Internal Audit, *Total Quality Auditing*® (TQA) was published in both book and workbook format in 2019 (entitled *Total Quality Audit: How a Total Quality Mindset Can Help Internal Audit Add Real Value*). She provides in-person and virtual CPE trainings regarding her TQA techniques, which have already been successfully implemented by many organizations.

Personally, Jo is known for her proactive nature as well. After finding out she was positive for the breast and ovarian cancer gene mutation (BRCA1) in 2015, Jo underwent multiple preventative surgeries, including a double mastectomy in 2016. She believes knowledge is power and encourages others to take action in their lives.

Jo's second book (also published in 2019 with an accompanying workbook), originally titled *Our Choices on the Road of Life,* was revised and re-published in 2021 titled, *Your Road. Your Choices.* The book begins with a look at her life story and explores how we can each make a choice to "embrace adversity." She also delivers several keynote presentations on our life choices, which have been called an *"epic experience."*

Jo's third book, *Becoming The Everyday Ethicist,* was published at the end of 2020. The book is based on Jo's personal and professional life experiences, her leadership experiences, and ethics research and studies. Jo is passionate about ethics and *Becoming The Everyday Ethicist* provides the keys to living an ethical life, shows leaders how to display integrity and earn trust, and demonstrates the importance of ethics (and ethics monitoring by Internal Auditors) in all organizations.

Jo has both her bachelor's and master's degrees in Accounting from the University of Georgia. She started her career in Public Accounting at one of the Big Four firms, experienced a traditional accounting role at a multinational corporation, and directed an Internal Audit function for ten years. She is also an Affiliate Faculty member at a State University in Colorado and has taught higher education courses including Principles of Accounting, Intermediate Accounting, Introduction to Business, and Internal Auditing.

Jo's experience includes advising management on a multitude of strategic initiatives, while providing ongoing recommendations for process and control improvements. She has designed SOX and other compliance programs, implemented audit management software suites, and has performed and managed financial, operational, and compliance audits for a multitude of industries, including oilfield services, agriculture, cannabis, transportation, insurance, retirement, investment, healthcare, higher education, and government. She has extensive risk assessment experience and focuses her efforts on what is critical for organizational success. She greatly enjoys working with her clients today on identifying and assessing their current and future risks.

Jo is an active member and instructor for the Colorado Society of CPAs (COCPAs) as well as a member of the Institute of Internal Auditors (IIA) and the Association of Certified Fraud Examiners (ACFE). Jo is currently serving as the Vice President of Academic Relations for the Denver Chapter of the

IIA. Jo is also a Professional Member of the National Speakers Association, at both the state and national level. On a more personal note, Jo is a Leadership Committee member and active volunteer with Susan G. Komen Colorado.

Contact:

Jo@AuditConsultingEducation.com

www.auditconsultingeducation.com

Follow on LinkedIn:

https://www.linkedin.com/in/amanda-jo-erven-ace/

https://www.linkedin.com/company/audit-consulting-education-llc

Comments About "Jo"

"What a privilege it is to know Jo and hear her story. Jo was one of our top-rated speakers in 2018... and will be invited back in 2019. Jo's authenticity, honesty, and candor are refreshing and genuine. Her ability to share her journey in a transferable way to a room of CPAs is a gift and an inspiration. Jo has enriched the lives of many..."

"It is people like (Jo) who show the world that what may seem impossible or otherwise inescapable – isn't."

"Jo is a passionate and thoughtful leader who is not afraid to take action to drive positive change. Her ability to understand the needs of a business and to navigate and resolve difficult situations makes her an asset wherever she is. My career has greatly benefitted from the guidance and insight Jo has given me. On a more personal note, Jo is someone who has dealt with real adversity in her life, and her ability to persevere and come out on top is incredibly impressive."

"Jo is a driven leader in her field and truly passionate in the development of others. She fosters a culture of constant improvement through mentorship and training to realize the highest potential from her team and bring value to clients and business partners. Her enthusiasm for learning and the development of others is second to none."

"Jo is a passionate leader who truly cares about her people. She is committed to her work and is dedicated to developing and mentoring her team. Jo is smart, efficient, and full of

energy. She inspires the team and drives to achieve goals effortlessly."

"Jo is honest, bringing high integrity to all she does. She has the courage of her convictions and is one that always does the right thing."

"Ethics implies trust. Jo sets this tone because her career demonstrates she knows how to build it."

"Jo takes responsibility for her actions and believes in meeting or exceeding her commitments. Her behavior and results-oriented approach forms the foundation upon which people can place their trust."

"Jo is personable and approachable; she builds great relationships, treats others with respect, and earns the respect of others."

A
BRAND
NEW ME

<u>The Purple Heart Mysteries</u>

THE PURPLE HEART DETECTIVE AGENCY

PRINCE OF THE BORDER

BABYLON BLUES

A BRAND NEW ME

FRIENDS / FIENDS WITH BENEFITS

A
BRAND
NEW ME

A Purple Heart Mystery

Rock Neelly

POST MORTEM PRESS
CINCINNATI

Post Mortem Press Cincinnati, OH

www.postmortem-press.com

FIRST EDITION

ISBN: 978-1975807047

A Brand New Me

He had predator eyes. Dangerous eyes that blinked laconically as they scrutinized me. He didn't speak after we shook hands and I waved him into my office. We walked side-by-side from the lobby to my office. I could hear the morning traffic on Figueroa below us, L.A. commuters arriving late to work. I studied him as he studied me. I watched those eyes seemingly take inventory of everything in the room. His darting eyes had thick, hooded lids as they danced, but his wide, tan face was impassive. His eyes didn't fit. They were in direct contrast to the rest of him.

He had that downtown uptight asshole businessman look down pat, except for the eyes, and unfortunately for him, they were the feature everyone would immediately notice and remember. They were animalistic green running to a jaundiced yellow. Those eyes revealed a malignance that the rest of him could not hide. They were an uncivilized vestige on an otherwise normal visage. Like noticing a panther's eyes peering out of your rose garden, a place that seemed tame a moment ago. The Brooks Brothers suit wasn't fooling anyone.

Roddy, my partner, arrived through the front door just as the client and I left the foyer. I sat behind the desk; the client sat facing me. Roddy, dressed in jeans, white Dodgers tee, and a blue blazer, waved a hello from the doorway. He attended to the coffeemaker on the credenza behind his desk in the lobby. He poured each of us a cup and entered the office on his mechanical legs. After handing the steaming mugs to both of us, my partner sat, reached out and shook the man's hand.

"Roddy O'Malley," he said.

"Calvin Grabber."

I noticed the man's grip was tight on Roddy's hand. I almost grinned. No one in their right mind would try to out squeeze Roddy in a handshake. My partner surreptitiously gave me a

raised eyebrow and a micro-grin. Roddy withdrew his hand rather than start a grip contest with a client.

Calvin Grabber's build was big, but not as massive as Roddy's. Then again nearly no one's was. My partner's upper body might give professional athletes pause, but the man who sat in front of me, now taking a sip of coffee, would be a handful. I put him at not quite 40, perhaps 6-1, with a thin waist but full shoulders. I get paid to notice details. I noticed this man had uncommonly thick wrists and a thick neck. His narrowed hips and legs were in contrast to arms that when flexed, tightened the sleeves of his expensive suitcoat. I would say we were in the presence of a man who lifted a lot of free weights. Stretched over his thick left wrist, his watch was thin and expensive. His cleft chin was set and his jaw locked in this awkward moment of silence, like we were playing chicken on who would speak first. I hoped we wouldn't have to play the staring game too.

Grabber seemed used to getting his way and he was used to order. I gauged his yellow-tinged eyes and his flat top haircut again, thinking he might be ex-military like us. Finally, he raised his hands, tipping them outward like "What's the hold-up?"

I blinked, wondering if I had misread his silence as a power ploy when it was instead a tacit insistence on a protocol he believed was to be followed in these kinds of matters—whatever matter these kind were.

"How can we help you, ah, Mr. Graber? I said in my best client friendly tone, messing with his name on purpose for no reason I could enunciate.

"No," he corrected, "it's Grabber. Calvin Grabber. Two B's. Common mistake."

I nodded, trying again. "Okay, Mr. Grabber, how can the Purple Heart Detective Agency help you?"

"I need you to find my wife and daughter. They've taken off."

I nodded again. Roddy leaned in and interjected, "When you say took off, you mean your wife took your daughter of her own volition, your wife's, I mean. Your wife bugged out with your little girl?"

"Yes, so far as I know," Grabber said, moving his chin up and down in a barely perceptible nod. "On her own volition as you call

it. She left me and took my ten-year-old with her. We'd had some fights, fights about money. My wife's mother just died and left her a fairly healthy sum. We were in disagreement about how to handle it properly."

"I see," I said. "If I may ask, how much?"

"Nearly a half million," he responded, blinking, "and it cleared probate just about two months ago. But before it did, she opened her own account at a different bank. I'm on the Board of Trustees at Herold's Financial in Burbank. Own my own financial investment business. Very solid. But she opened another account unbeknownst to me. Had the money sent there." He looked down and saw the coffee cup in his hand. Almost startled, he acknowledged it with a sip. "Without my prior knowledge," he added.

"Without your prior knowledge," I repeated, taking stock. I likewise took a sip, letting the steam go past my nose. "Maybe not an easy thing to see your wife do, but it is certainly within her legal claim, I would suppose."

"Embarrassing, yes." He nodded, but his eyes flared a bit, illuminating the yellow in them. He would be a bad poker player. "Yes, within her rights, but leaving with not a word and taking our daughter is not." He looked at the both of us as if his head was on a swivel back and forth. "Not within her rights." His eyes lit yellow with animation.

"And you want us to find them?" Roddy asked. My partner stood and pointed to his cup. "Heat up, anyone?"

Grabber and I both shook our heads no. Roddy strolled out of the office to the reception area back to the coffee machine. However, he was not after coffee; he was sending me a text. We had done this before. I peeked down at my phone which lay visible only to me in my barely open center drawer. I gazed down. "Creep" was the one word message. I nodded slightly as Roddy reentered the room.

Roddy said, "Here's the deal, Mr. Grabber. We don't do a lot of domestic work these days. What brought you to us? There are lots of firms in Los Angeles that specialize in this kind of work."

Grabber turned in his chair to address Rod. He set his mug on my desk and gripped the arms of his chair. The leather stretched

tight under his powerful fingers. "I read about you guys. The detectives with only one leg between the two of you. How you're willing to bend the rules for a client here and there, but you're discrete. Client friendly in the extreme."

"We don't break the law, Mr. Grabber," I said.

He smiled, cocking one eyebrow in the air. "That's not how I heard it. But okay. I don't need you to break any laws. I just want the two of them found. I need to know they're okay. I want my daughter back at home."

"And your wife?" I asked.

Grabber's eyes blazed a citrine blond fire. Poison leaked into his words without his wanting it to. "If she wants to come home, she's welcome. It's her home too."

"How long they been gone?"

"A month," he paused, "or so."

Neither Roddy nor I spoke, but we exchanged looks. A month? Or so? They had been missing for a month? Mr. Grabber could read our faces. "Before you judge me, hear me out. Candace, my wife, deceived me. They were to have gone on a mission-trip to Utah. To help at a bible camp on an Indian Reservation. I got postcards from one or the other of them nearly every day." He brought out the cards and passed them to us with a photo of the wife and also the daughter. "Then on the day of their return, I went to the church to pick them up to find that my wife had cancelled at the last moment. Didn't give the sponsors any reason, but paid for their stay anyway. They'd been gone for four weeks before I knew they were missing. Must have had someone help them mail the cards to me. The postmarks are all from Utah." I wondered if the man's fingers were going to tear into my chair's leather. His grip finally loosened, but only a bit. I could see his hands tremble with anger.

Roddy leaned his head back as he sat down beside Grabber once more. As the man turned his eyes back to me, Roddy raised his brows and mouthed "Wow." Only I saw it.

I said, "Tell you what, Mr. Grabber. We can do this much. We'll find 'em. Make sure they're okay, but I don't think we're telling you where they are. That'll be up to your wife if she chooses to do so."

He stared at me, red-tint started to run up his neck. "That's not..."

I interrupted him. "We'll find them and talk to them. Make sure they are okay. Tell them you are worried. That you want your daughter back home. If you want to go so far as to file a missing person's report, then when we find them we would be compelled to tell the police where they are. You would then find out your family's location through the cops. But we're not going to bloodhound your wife and daughter for you. We're not dragging them back home for you and we're not going to find them and bring you to them to allow you to drag them home by force either."

Grabber's face was red. His eyes bore into me with enmity.

"Otherwise," I added, "you'll need to find another firm." His face stayed red, his eyes yellow, but he nodded he agreed to the terms.

Roddy leaned toward Grabber, putting his one hand on my desk. "It's a thousand a day, three days minimum. Plus expenses. Need you to fill out the standard contract—Grace, give him one—and we'll need a retainer as well. At least a grand up front."

Grabber squinted at Roddy with narrowed eyes. He removed a folded cashier's check for ten thousand dollars from his suit's vest pocket. He smoothed the crease with diligence, placed it on the desk next to his coffee cup and said in a harsh, almost wolfish whisper, "No police. You just find 'em. Report back only to me. We clear on that?" His eyes moved from Roddy to me.

I nodded.

"Where's that contract?"

I opened the side drawer and handed him the single sheet of paper.

* * * * *

When Grabber had gone, Roddy laughed out loud. "What a dildo, eh?"

I looked back at him. "Actually I thought he was a little scary." I peered down at the client's two photographs before me, one of the wife, the other of the daughter. I picked up the wife's image.

Candace Grabber was a milquetoast of a woman, mousy blonde hair cut shoulder length and pushed behind her ears. Her

chin was quite weak and ruined her looks. In the photo, she tucked her chin down toward her chest like she was trying to hide her miserable jawline, but instead it made her upper teeth jut forward, and she frowned in the photo in a failed attempt to hide those choppers. She was a small breasted woman with a flat stomach and narrow hips. Her clothes were Southern California Catholic. Loose and conservative. Her eyes were, like her husband's, her most interesting feature. They were like a wren's. Birdlike and inquisitive. Perhaps secretive.

I wondered how secretive. After all, she had gone off the grid with half a million bucks. That kind of dough could create the need for lots of secrets. I said, "Hubby said before he left his wife really only goes to church on Wednesday and Sunday, to Von's Groceries on Saturday morning, and to the rectory for lunches on Fridays. No known associates other than church ladies."

Roddy likewise examined the little girl's photo. "Sherri Grabber, aged 10," he said. "Daddio says she gonna be in fourth grade. Smart and highly, almost fervently, religious. Goes to the local Catholic parochial school. Her father, as you heard, says she's never had a girl from school to their home and to his knowledge has not been to a sleep-over. So I'm guessing she's not popular with her classmates."

"Dysfunctional parents are such a drag," I opined. "How you want to break things up?"

"You take the school, the church, the rectory. I'll take the house, the computers, the phones. Interview Mr. Sunshine again."

"Okay," I said. "You think mom and daughter are long gone?"

Rod laughed. "Yeah, finding 'em's a million to one shot."

"Nah," I said, "half a million."

* * * * *

That afternoon, we split up and I headed to the rectory first, then the church. The nuns were not much help. The priests less. The former assured me Mrs. Grabber was a pious woman given to contemplation, solitude, and prayer. The priests seemed more aware Mr. Grabber was good for a tithe on a rather large income each year and gave even more during the season of Lent. The good fathers had no ill words to say about the family. I found one priest,

Father Bregoli outside the living quarters of the clergy as he knelt in a tomato garden on the back lawn He casually wore a white tee and dark gray trousers and I questioned him as he weeded, crawling from row to row. After he gave me nothing to go on, I asked him, "What about in the confessional? Anything that might indicate Mrs. Grabber might suddenly take a powder? Make a run for it? Anything about the husband that might make her want to get away?"

Father Bregoli tugged a blood red, beef steak tomato from the vine, looking up at me in the bright Southern California sun. "The confessional is a place where secrets are safe. I am sworn to silence. The penitent's confession is sacrosanct. It is part of the sacrament. Did you not know that?"

"Yeah," I said, "I was raised in the Church but no longer attend. I know those confessions are secret, but we might be talking about saving a woman's life. And her daughter's. There is a child to consider."

"We are all children in the eyes of the Lord. How long since you last confessed your sins, Mr. err? I'm sorry. I forgot your name."

"Grace."

He raised an eyebrow as he raised from all fours to his knees. "Grace eh? Remember the meaning of your name. His grace is necessary for your salvation. How long since you were in confession, Mr. Grace?"

"Too long, but I'm afraid it's not in the cards for today. I've got a missing woman and girl to find," I countered, begging off.

The priest shook his head. "I cannot help you in your search. I know nothing that would aid your finding them." And then the priest tossed a sticky tomato to me, his eye squinting into the brightness of the day. "Churches do not run on faith alone. Mr. Grabber is a generous parishioner. You don't get blood from a turnip."

I tossed the tomato, which had ruptured, back to him, juice staining my sleeve. "The similarity in saving souls and saving lives should not be confused with the money to be made in the process," I said and walked away not waiting for a reaction.

The rest of the day was a washout. No news and no one told me anything helpful. Later while reviewing my notes, I decided perhaps the only person who might know more than she was saying was the receptionist at the church. I interviewed her in front of a priest and two of the nuns who did clerical work there. She followed their lead and clammed up. That was a tactical mistake and I would follow up with her again. Afterwards I called Roddy. He was just on the way home.

"How'd it go? You speak to Grabber again?"

"Yeah," Rod laughed, "went to the house. Bel Air address, but not so as you would know it. Bel Air by zip code only. A 1960's bi-level—big and outdated. Seems to have been in the family forever. Furniture is strictly Grandma heirloom—if your granny was Liberace. And listen to this, Grabber, that sick fuck, had a key stroke recording device on the home desktop to keep tabs on what websites his wife visited and what emails she received."

"And?"

"No smoking gun. Nothing much to see. She only had restricted access to the internet. Grabber locked his office when he went to work. Even during the evenings and weekends when Candace did have access, there wasn't anything interesting. Maybe the wife knew she was being spied on with the keystroke device. There is one thing of note. During approved hours of usage, she visited a non-profit called A Brand New Me a couple of times. It's a place that caters to women fallen upon hard times. Gets them work clothes when they are planning on getting back into the work force, helps them learn to interview for employment. That sort of thing."

I pondered his comment. "Hmm, now that you mention it, I think the receptionist at the church was trying damn hard not to look at a poster for that place on the church office bulletin board. We may have ourselves a lead. Shall we head down there tomorrow morning?"

"Yeah, wanna meet me in the morning at Malibu Farm Pier Café?"

I said, "Sure, you go early and get a table."

* * * * *

The next morning after breakfast, we pulled into the parking lot, Roddy removed a soft-sided messenger bag out from under the seat. He slipped a device from the flap and set it on the seat.

"What's that?" I asked.

"It's called a Stingray," Roddy replied, "at least in FBI lingo, it's called that."

"And it does what?"

"It's a fake cell phone tower. Creates an extra strong beacon to cell phones in the area, so strong it draws them in to this particular beacon. More so than a typical triangulated signal."

"And then?" I asked, Roddy making me beg for more of his techie talk.

"Then any cell phone in the direct vicinity will send its signal through my fake beacon. The call will still go through, but my Stingray will record all connections made. Phone number to phone number."

I nodded. "Does it record the conversation?"

Roddy shook his head. "The FBI version does. Mine is not sophisticated enough to do that. But it does let us know who calls who. We can see if someone inside A Brand New Me makes a call after we leave."

"Ah," I said, getting it. "So we see who's next up the food chain. Maybe someone will call Candace Grabber after we leave."

Roddy nodded. "If someone inside there," he pointed with his chin to the front door, "knows anything about the Grabber's disappearance and calls a co-conspirator, we'll know. Otherwise, we just see where they're ordering takeout."

"And if the guilty party uses a landline?"

"We're screwed."

* * * * *

A Brand New Me was at the end of a strip mall full of dentists, dermatologists, and dry cleaners. It looked a little run-down-at-the-heels, but the receptionist was friendly enough and within a few minutes showed us into an office where the lead counselor for the organization offered us coffee from one of those machines that makes one cup at a time. It tasted of hard water and hazelnut. I

explained our mission to find both Mrs. Candace Grabber and her daughter, Sherri. The counselor nodded with concern.

"I know Candace Grabber," said the head counselor, a Ms. Sandy Jenkins. She was a dishwater blonde of about 35, slim and put together, tiny tits, no bra. I liked her at first handshake, but she wasn't helpful. She was a true believer, it seemed, in whatever she believed. Friendly, lots of smiles, but no go on info. But she did throw us a bone at the end of our questions.

"I'm sorry I can't help you find Mrs. Grabber. She's a good person. Candace was a volunteer here."

"Volunteer?" I echoed.

"Yes, she read practice interview questions to some of our clients. We serve women who have difficult home lives. Often the victims of domestic violence. Women who are often now homeless, living in shelters. Many times, they have never worked, having been stay-at-home moms. Candace helped women practice their interview skills and helped them create resumes before applying for jobs. But she's only been assisting for a couple of months."

Roddy nodded. "And you know all the volunteers?"

Ms. Jenkins smiled as she shook her head no. "Oh no, we have lots of people who help out. They come and go. But I remember Candace because she donated some money last month. Wrote us a check for $1,000. I stopped by and personally thanked her. She seemed embarrassed by the additional attention."

I looked to Roddy. "Makes sense. Right after she came into her money."

"How many people work here?" I asked.

Ms. Jenkins said, "Full-time? Just four of us. But we have probably 40 volunteers at any one time. Businesswomen, doctors, psychiatrists, social workers, and lots of church women. Some men help too, of course." She smiled to let us know she was being nice, but her look told us not many men passed through these doors—and fewer still were trusted.

"Do you have any idea where Candace Grabber and her daughter might have gone? Or know of anyone here who might have assisted her?"

Ms. Jenkins kept up her perky mood, but offered no assistance. "No," she said, "I only spoke to her personally that one time. I'm sorry I can't help."

* * * * *

We returned to the truck afterwards and saw the data bank growing from the Stingray collecting cell phone calls from the building in front of us. We waited an hour, watching the data flow in, then headed back to the office. But analyzing the data would have to wait. When we returned to Third and Figueroa, Calvin Grabber stood outside our locked office door.

"I want a status report," he said, following as we entered.

My partner gave me a bob of the head, raising the messenger bag containing the Stingray like "you handle this shit" and skedaddled on into the office. He closed the door. I heard the lock click behind him.

Grabber moved in close to my face. Too close. "Where's he going? What's in that bag?"

I wanted to push the man back, but kept it under control and moved around Roddy's desk, creating some space between us. "It's only been one day. We've been interviewing your wife's known associates. Roddy's examined her emails, her bank statements, your phone records. We may have something, but it's too early in the investigation…"

Calvin Grabber cut me off. "What have you got? Who helped her get away?" His face was red. He put those thick wrists of his down on the desk and leaned toward me. His eyes glowed.

I leaned right back into him. My face nearly touched his. "We got nothin'. Not yet."

"I gave you ten thousand dollars. I demand to know what you have so far." He did not intimidate easily, but nor did I. Roddy would laugh at the scene if he came back into the room.

I took a breath, giving in, but with my point made. "That's not the terms we agreed to. We're not hunting them down for you to drag home. We don't know where they are or even who helped them—if someone did. We might have a lead. That's what Roddy's working on right now. We're good at this. Keep the faith."

Grabber stood up, his point likewise made. "Will you call me this evening to let me know if your lead panned out?"

"Sure," I said and motioned toward the door.

Grabber nodded solemnly and exited without another word.

* * * * *

I entered my office after a knock and an unlocking twist to the knob on Roddy's side. "Got anything?"

"Maybe. The perky Sandy Jenkins made two calls in the first five minutes after we left. I'm checking them right now. But it appears the first was to a cosmetic surgeon on Rodeo Drive."

"That's interesting," I said, moving to the desk, adjusting my prosthesis by propping it on the surface as I sat down.

Roddy peered up from his laptop as he used the police reverse phone number directory software he'd stolen. "Second phone call is even more interesting."

"Really? Pray tell, who?"

"LAPD Domestic Violence Major Assault Unit. Hollenbeck Division. Detective named Marla Young."

"A cop?"

"Yeah, a cop."

* * * * *

The next morning we went to see the plastic surgeon, a Dr. Anthony Maglioni, but he was in surgery and was not expected to be free for at least four hours. We decided on a trip to the Hollenbeck Division to see Detective Marla Young. She was out and otherwise occupied, but after finding out I had spent seven years on the force, the desk sergeant made a call on our behalf. We met her at a watering hole on South Spring called Crane's where cops went for lunch. Cool place. The bar was set up in an old bank vault. During daylight hours it was a quiet joint. It looked like Detective Young might know her way around the vault bar here a bit too well. Her face was rosy and her eyes suspicious as we met her near a tabletop poker machine.

Roddy analyzed the situation well. He pulled up a stool and ordered a cold draw and a Jack chaser. He nodded at her, gave her a wink, and surprisingly she responded back with a nod. He waved

his finger around and the bartender brought three of each. I plotted out how to question her, but it turned out Detective Marla Young was an easy nut to crack. She wanted to get drunk, or so it seemed. And more than that, she seemed eager to get her secret off her chest.

"A Brand New Me isn't really about helping women interview for a job. That is a front," the detective told us within 15 minutes and two drinks. She'd been drinking before we arrived, I could tell, and whatever she was hiding was eating her up inside. Young almost begged us to listen to her story. "It's all by word of mouth. Women who need to get away from their men. You know the type. Controlling assholes. Batterers. Abusers. But for the women we help, these assholes usually have enough money and influence to keep them from getting on with their lives. Lots of sad women trying to ditch bad guys."

I noticed the "we" in her description. "And Candace Grabber decided to make use of the organization's services?" I asked.

"Yes."

"How's it work?" Roddy asked. He started to motion for more drinks. I stopped him. I thought Detective Young was too intoxicated already. I was worried with another drink she wouldn't get the details to us correctly.

"There are women who support the program," she said. "Older rich women, so there is money. We use the money to find women who are in hospitals or hospices. A Brand New Me recruits women who have terminal diseases, like cancer or advanced lupus."

Roddy asked, "How do these dying women help? Do you scam them out of their money?"

Detective Young looked at him with a slanted eye. "No, we scam them out of their names."

And then she spilled the beans. It was like her confession was held back by the slenderest of dams, like the membrane on the brim of an overfull pint of beer before the fluid leaks over the side. The tiniest breech could cause a major spill. We couldn't have stopped her telling us the story if we wanted to.

Marla Young met Sandy Jenkins, the head counselor at A Brand New Me several years ago when the detective brought some abused women to the nonprofit for help. The organization initially

provided assistance to women in finding new homes, new employment and self-respect. Prior to Detective Young's involvement, most of the organization's clients were in the city's homeless shelters, but the policewoman began to bring A Brand New Me a new type of client—an affluent one, but still one who was abused and in need of assistance. Over drinks one night, Young and Jenkins created a hypothetical "underground railroad" for the abused women. When the two sobered up the next day, the idea percolated. Then in the week after, a client was killed by her husband after he found she'd received a suit of clothes from A Brand New Me. The abused woman's plan was to get a job and leave her husband. He did not allow her that chance. Suddenly, the percolation became a real plan.

Perky Sandy Jenkins was in sales. She developed scouts who found women in hospice or hospital care who were terminally ill and without family attending to them. The counselor assembled a number of recruiters in the Los Angeles area hospice community to seek these lonely survivors out. It sounds impossible, but that's not true, said the female detective. There are 18 million people in the greater Los Angeles area. Of that, perhaps one percent die each year—most of natural causes. Of that 18,000, roughly 8,500 are female. Most are elderly. Of those, 90 percent have family by their side, but still just under 100 each year, Sandy Jenkins discovered, were terminally ill and on their own. It was to these women each year that A Brand New Me's' underground railroad reached out.

The play was sweet. These dying women could give the gift of life to another woman, one who needed a new start, a new identity. The terminally ill women must agree to die anonymously as a ward of the state—which was a short step from the death they were currently facing.

If the woman agreed, she was moved to the city's hospice for the medically indigent. Her intake papers said "Jane Doe." She was listed as suffering from dementia, no identity available, having been found by police on the streets. The police, in each case, was, of course, Detective Marla Young. Each indigent woman was given a medical work-up. The diagnosis was already known to be terminal. Each was placed in the hospice with a wink and a nod. The now indigent woman would die with dignity, knowing her

name would live on with another woman, one running from her abusive husband or partner. The ole switcho-chango.

That was step one. Step two was the client, who was now on the run and might be considered missing or the victim of foul play, would be hidden in a safe house. Off the radar. Then step three would be put into play. The client would receive cosmetic surgery, altering her facial features and even providing liposuction or breast augmentation. Stylists were brought into the safe house to provide new hair colors, new cuts, and a new look after sufficient healing had taken place after the cosmetic surgery. Personal shoppers provided new clothing. No expense was spared; no vestige of the client's past was allowed to remain.

Step four was the use of a forger to provide an updated driver's license with a photo of the client's new face. The social security card of the deceased was still good as her death had gone unreported. Usually the credit of the previous owner of the identity had been strained by the medical bills of the terminally ill, but there were the other benefactors who pledged money to this women's underground railroad. The few who were recruited while still having some assets gave them to the organization.

When Marla Young finished her tale, Roddy bought her one more beer. Her mouth seemed dry and her lips parched from so much talking.

I nodded at her. "And then where do they go? These women you set up for a new life? You just let them walk out the door?"

Marla shook her head. "Most I take down to LAX and put on a plane. One-way ticket purchased with cash."

"And you never hear from them again?" Roddy asked.

"There is an email address Sandy monitors to see if any of them need help. We generally don't hear from them again."

Roddy mused for a second. "How many we talking about over the last three years?"

"Maybe five the first year as we were learning the ropes," said Detective Young. "We moved slow, made sure we got everything right. The next two years 20. Nine the second, and eleven the third. We're just beginning our fourth year of spiriting these women away."

"Who signs the death certificates on the Jane Does?" I asked.

Detective Young narrowed her eyes. "A woman at the county morgue processes for us. She doesn't ask too many questions as long as the cause of deaths prove to be natural."

"She doesn't know the scam?"

"Doesn't know, but has probably figured it out. Didn't need it spelled out."

"And how do the women get moved to the indigent care unit?

"Ambulance service. Same folks every time. A Brand New Me has them on retainer. We pay well. It's on the up-and-up. Other than that the intake papers are switched at the pick-up. Sandy Jenkins takes care of the switch."

"After the forger does the paperwork?" I chimed in.

"Nah, intakes are easy. Just typed two page forms. Sometimes I fill them out. Sometimes Sandy."

"And the cosmetic work? Another man-hater wanting to help her sister?" I asked, killing the last of my beer.

Detective Young laughed. "You're a cynical bastard."

"Seven years on the force, three wearing the shield, vice and homicide."

She nodded. "That explains the cynicism."

Roddy steered her back. "So, you've helped 25 women go off the grid? Accessory before the fact on 25, including the creation of forged legal documents. Faked another 25 death certificates. Defrauded the state of out of hospice and burial expenses for 25 women. Lied to investigating officers, I'm sure, probably the FBI too, again illegal. Filed false police reports. Grace here is better than me at knowing what charges could get filed. I'm sure he could add on for a while."

"You're saying I would be in jail a long time if the shit comes down."

Roddy nodded.

She nodded back. "Before I ask you if it's gonna rain shit today, let me tell you this. I'd do it again. I've worked this job for 23 years. Been on Domestic Abuse for eight years. Saw a lot of women killed by their partners. Murder. Murder/suicide. Murder, death by cop. In the last three years, I saved 25 lives." She looked to me. "You know for sure you saved 25 lives in your career? I do. For damned sure, I do." She placed her fist on the bar.

I shook my head slowly. "Not 25. Not for sure."

Her eyes turned a deeper brown as she raised her face to the two of us. "Should I expect a shit storm? I always knew there might come a day of retribution for breaking my oath of 'Protect and Serve. I'm prepared for it."

Roddy shook his head. "Don't think you broke it, lady. We only promised we would find Candace Grabber. We never promised her schmuck of a husband we would tell him where she was. We just need to make sure she and her daughter are okay."

I stuck out my hand. "Thanks for your service to the city, Detective Young."

"Thanks." Her voice broke and her eyes filled with tears.

"Four things," I said as we both rose to leave. "One, where did Candace Grabber fly off to with her one-way ticket? Two, what name is she going by? And three, what is the name of the cosmetic surgeon you used for Candace Grabber?"

Detective Young raised her chin a bit. "She was the only one who didn't leave L.A. She wanted to live a new life right under the nose of that son-of-a-bitch husband of hers. She just got in a taxi with her daughter and rode away. I got no clue where she is. And since I didn't book the plane ticket, I never got a name either."

Roddy nodded. "The plastic surgeon's name?"

"Anthony Maglioni on Rodeo Drive."

"We thought as much. Only the best, eh?" I said.

"He charges us next to nothing and then writes off the entire amount off in taxes. Ten of 'em a year, he says, and then he pays squat to Uncle Sam in taxes."

Roddy laughed. "We'll add Accessory to Tax Evasion to the list." He turned to go.

Detective Young looked at me. "You said four things."

"Yeah," I said, "the last one's advice. Get into AA. You're too good a cop to go down the drain with booze."

She nodded. I took a step, then paused again. "You're not gonna give us Candace's new identity? I think you do know it. We're not going to jam you up. You know that, right?"

Detective Young smiled, waving the bartender over for a celebratory last round of her liquid lunch. "I swear I don't know it. I would have if I would have booked her a plane ticket. But she

didn't want one. We're on a need-to-know basis. Sandy would know."

I smiled. "Yeah, well, she's not telling."

Detective Young shrugged.

After sitting for an hour listening to the detective's tale, I limped on my good leg to the door. Sitting for so long had made my stump ache. I heard Detective Young call my name. "Grace, Detective Grace," She used the title I had not heard in so long.

"Yeah?" I thought she was going to give me the name.

"Be careful with Grabber. He may look like a banker, but he's a cruel, dangerous man. He did awful things to Candace before she left. But nothing we could prove in court. He's bad. Pure bad."

"Gotcha," I said into the daylight as I reentered the street, "I kind of figured that one out."

* * * * *

Roddy was behind the wheel of his hand controlled GMC truck when I joined him outside. A parking ticket was tucked under the windshield wiper. He opened the window, leaned way out, turned on the wiper and as the ticket rose with the blade, he grabbed it, wadded it up, and threw it into behind the seat of the truck in one motion.

"Not afraid they'll boot your truck for unpaid tickets?" I asked.

Roddy smiled, lighting a cigarette. "Nope, their software is easy to hack. I just go in and change the ticket over to paid. Easy-peezy."

I shook my head and laughed.

"Where to, Captain, oh Captain?" he asked, joining me.

I pointed west. "Rodeo Drive. Dr. Anthony Maglioni, cosmetic surgeon and tax evader."

"Thought you'd say that."

* * * * *

Dr. Maglioni's office was a single door leading off the street in the 200 block of North Rodeo Drive, not far from Agent Provocateur, a very upscale lingerie place. Roddy smiled as we passed it by, looking for a parking place. "You ever been in there?"

"No, why?"

"Karen got me something for my birthday from there."

"For you?"

"Well, she wore it, but yeah, it was for me."

"Getting close to TMI, Rod. But I'm happy for you. Karen is a keeper. Hey, look there, a handicapped parking spot."

Roddy expertly navigated into the space, pulled the permit from the side pocket in the door and hung it from the mirror. We ambled down the block, watching ever-so-thin women with augmented breasts leave the doctor's office and head into the lingerie store. We both smiled.

Maglioni made us wait for a bit, but then a male receptionist, tall, thin and snotty, led us to a paneled mahogany office. Maglioni was everything a cosmetic surgeon on Rodeo Drive should be—mannered, Italian accented, prosperous with a tiny speck of greed hanging from his sleeve. "Gentlemen, gentlemen, Silas gave me your cards. The Purple Heart Detective Agency. Who has not heard of you from the papers? What can I do for you?" The doctor gently shook our hands and directed us to sit in bright red chairs, the leather arms so soft the breasts he worked on would have seemed like sandpaper in comparison.

"We just had a long conversation with Detective Marla Young. She told us quite a story." Roddy was silent, letting me do the talking.

"I see. And you have questions for me?" The smile was gone off of Maglioni's face, but his composure was in place.

"Yes. We understand you are part of an 'underground railroad' type organization which is helping abused women set up new lives for themselves. You help them change their looks to evade their abusive spouses."

"I do nothing of the kind."

"Well, according to Detective Young," I started, but he cut me off.

"I do charitable work for A Brand New Me, an organization which helps abused women. They come to me with medical certificates from a licensed physician on staff there. I provide my services at cost, which are paid by donations to the non-profit. All of my actions are strictly above board."

"Except none of the women are using their real names."

"So you say." Maglioni smiled, taking some hand lotion from his desk and applying a tiny drop to each palm. He motioned to each of us if we should like some. We declined. "I assure you this conversation is the first time I have heard of such affairs. It sounds so like a conspiracy theory to me. Like a delicious movie plot, don't you think?"

"Not really. And we really don't care about your arrangement with the organization and any tax benefits you might get from working with them."

The good doctor blanched at that, but then shrugged it off. He did not respond.

"We're just looking for one woman. Mrs. Candace Grabber," Roddy said and leaned across the table and handed the good doctor her photo.

"Have you treated her?" Roddy asked.

"Classic overbite, weak chin. Poorly defined cheekbones. Easy fixes really."

"Yes, I'm sure," Roddy replied, "but did you work on her?"

"I'm sure," Maglioni said, his smile both effacing and deferential in tandem, "you are aware privacy laws forbid me from telling you anything about a patient's medical records—if Ms. Grabber was a patient, which I cannot confirm or deny."

"So, you're not giving us shit," Rod said with just a hint of hostility.

Maglioni smiled greasily. "Oh no," he laughed. "I think that's exactly what I'm giving you."

* * * * *

Afterwards, Roddy and I went to our favorite bar, Sundowners, a darkly paneled afterhours place with the longest running poker game in L.A. going on in the back. Our buddy Rat was already at the table, having arrived before we did. He waved, but his cards must have been good, because his sunglasses went right back down after he greeted us. He was into the game and it was how he earned his living so he'd better be into it.

We got a table off to ourselves. Roddy ordered a Widow Jane with a splash. "What the hell is that?" I asked.

"Good new bourbon. Made in Brooklyn."

"Because all the good bourbon is made in... Brooklyn. I'll take mine from Kentucky. Give me a Wellers," I said to the waitress who knew us but left us be after taking our orders.

Roddy smiled. I knew that smile. My partner had an idea. "What's in that brain pan of yours, compadre?" I asked.

Roddy didn't speak. He just sat there listening to the bar stereo play "In a Sentimental Mood" by Duke Ellington with John Coltrane on the sax. Roddy stayed just like that with a shit-eating grin on his face until our drinks arrived. He ordered a second round as she set them down. He sipped his first and then took a big swig.

"Spill it."

"No way. Do you have any idea how much this stuff costs?"

"Your idea, smart ass. Spill it."

Roddy smiled and spoke, his voice honey after the smooth whisky. "A Brand New Me is a non-profit. Probably a 501(c)(3). That means their donors are public record. We can check the names of the women who have donated to the organization. That list is likely to have the names of the dying women who were recruited to give up their identities. We can cross reference the names on the list to known addresses. Those who have obvious public records we eliminate. Those who do not, we track down their photo from California DMV. We'll use my bootleg FBI facial recognition software to try to establish a match between the photos on the driver's licenses of the women who now have those names and Candace Grabber's photo. See if we get a match."

"Any idea how many women might donate to A Brand New Me?"

"Not a clue, but I bet it's a lot. But the computer will do most of the work eliminating the wrong faces. We just run down the photos on those we can't find a virtual record for. Most people will have some shit on-line. Facebook, Twitter, you know, 21st century stuff." Roddy paused, "Oh no, I guess you wouldn't." He laughed. I am not very into tech and social media. He rarely lets me forget it.

Our second round of drinks arrived and we took our time. Rat came over with some winnings and bought a third round. Then

Roddy waved us off. "Now I'm too drunk to drive us home. I'm a father now, you know. Can't go around driving drunk."

Rat smiled. "That was my first. I'll take you."

Since Karen was gone with the baby visiting her parents in Scottsdale, I also crashed at Roddy's place for the night. An hour and a pizza later, Karen called with her nose a little out of joint after Roddy answered the phone drunk (we drank a couple more once we arrived at the house), but she complemented Rod on catching a ride home while intoxicated and decided it was a step toward maturity. A truce was declared and the conversation, at least the portion I heard, became less accusatory. "Baby steps, baby," he was telling her as he carried phone up the stairs, cooing at her. Then I slid off to my home away from home, the spare bedroom, and slept.

* * * * *

When I woke up, it looked as if Roddy had been working on his computer most of the night. He sat in boxer shorts at the kitchen island, pounding away at the keyboard. He did not look up as I entered. "I'll have something for us in about two hours. You'll need to go after one of our vehicles. Mine is at the bar. Yours is at the office. There's a twenty by the coffee maker. Get a dozen donuts at Blinkie's Donut Emporium on Topanga Canyon Blvd before you come back."

I saluted him. "Aye-aye, Captain."

Roddy looked up, laughing.

"You sure you weren't an officer back in over in the sandbox?" I asked. "You sure sound like a brass ass."

"Sorry, I'm on a roll. I downloaded the annual reports and the monthly addendums from A Brand New Me. I found a list of quite a lot of women donors. I'm cross-referencing them against new driver's licenses issued. Also, I'm checking any social media for photos of the women before and after the issuance of driver's licenses. Also checking medical records. Then eliminating any women whose records were issued before Candace went missing. Then I'll use her photo as the template for a facial recognition program with all the women in the database of the non-profit. I will again cross-reference that program with all the photos. Then

we'll see if we can narrow the list down. Right now I've got about three hundred donors. I have no idea if it will work or if we'll get anyone who looks even a little bit like Candace Grabber."

I nodded, kind of getting it. "And if we figure out a name, we'll have a leg up on finding her. If—and that is a big 'if'—she is still in Southern California. It could be she didn't trust Detective Marla Young to keep her mouth shut about her destination."

"Which would have shown pretty good instincts as it turns out," Rod replied.

"Yep," I agreed. "It would have. Maybe Candace, with her new name, took a bus to San Diego and bought a one-way ticket for the two of them to Toledo, Ohio."

"And if she did that, we got pretty much no shot. Not if they're living off the grid. Living on cash."

"And she's got a ton of freaking cash."

Roddy's eyes went back to the laptop screen. "So, go get us some wheels and don't come back without the donuts.

"Sir, yes, sir." I grabbed the twenty off the bar and headed out the door, dialing Uber as I went. The morning was nice and I would sit outside for my ride.

* * * * *

Uber dropped me at the office. I went up to check mail and messages before getting the jeep and heading back to Roddy's. The phone on the desk rang as I entered.

"Get those bloodstains off your cuffs?" said the voice, a male's.

"Who is this?"

"I'm sorry. It's Father Bregoli. I'm afraid I made a bad joke— you know the tomato juice. Your comeback stung me the other day. I guess I brushed you off a bit harshly. And now that appears to have been a bad mistake."

"Oh, hello," I replied. "A bad mistake? Why?"

"Well, Calvin Grabber just called. It appears he is at A Brand New Me raising... well, raising a ruckus, and now he's headed our way. He sounded quite angry. Perhaps violently so. I was thinking of calling the police, but I still had your card and thought of calling you first."

"Okay, if he's raising hell before I get there, do call the cops. Don't take a chance. I'm in my office right now, but I'll hurry. I'm a bit closer to you than Grabber probably is right now. I'm on my way."

It took only 20 minutes to the rectory since I ran some lights and raced way over the speed limit, but Grabber beat me there. I could hear his bellow from the foyer of the rectory office as I entered.

"You. You're her best friend," he shouted. "It was either you who helped her or you know who did. I know you did. I'm sure of it." Grabber's voice was thick with malevolence. I stepped inside the door of the office. The beefy man was doing his lean-over-the-desk intimidation trick. He towered over the receptionist like a red-eyed vulture. His voice was tremulous and full of menace. "Tell me, damn it," he said.

I interceded, motioning with my hand for him to join me in the hallway. I decided to play a bluff, to give Grabber a red herring to grab onto, remembering something in the reports Roddy put together after examining the family's computer. "Mr. Grabber, a word please."

He looked at me, confused that I should be there. "Not now. They know something and they're not telling. They must..."

I interrupted him. "Roddy and I have a real lead. We found someone who's seen them," I lied.

His head turned, though his frame stayed over the desk, leaning into the frightened woman's face. "What?"

"In the hall?" I said, turning my back, leaving the antechamber.

He joined me red-faced. "'What have you learned?"

"Did you take a woman to Palm Desert? Last winter, did you take a woman, not your wife, to Palm Desert?"

Grabber looked dumbfounded. "No, of course not. I did go there. I went there for a conference last winter, but I was alone."

"But you stayed offsite? Casa Larrea Inn or something like that? Ordered wine to your room? Like you were socializing."

"Yes, that hotel was cheaper than the conference resort rate by quite a lot. I met another member of the board there. He wanted

wine. I did not object. And what has wine to do with my wife's disappearance?"

"Candace was seen in several women's apparel stores in the Beverly Center Mall. She was buying resort wear, swimsuits, tennis garb, like that. We canvassed with Candace's and your daughter's photos. Several clerks remembered her. Large purchases for cash, headed to Palm Desert. She saw your hotel bill. Candace said she was going to see if she could find the bimbo you were with, to use her words. Said 'two can play at that game.'" I laid it on thick. "Did she get it wrong? Did you not have a woman with you up there?"

Grabber was stunned. "Of course not. I told you. It was a financial conference. Our annual state meeting. We always have it at a resort out of season. I was with Dennis Malone. Candace knows him quite well. Oh my God. Do you think she's up there right now?"

"We have a man canvassing the various resorts with their photos," I fibbed. "There are a lot of the hotels out there and if she's paying cash, there'll be no record. Most of the best places are very discreet, so people aren't going to talk."

"Did you try Casa Larrea?"

"Yeah, she's not there."

Grabber looked perplexed. I realized then he may have been up late drinking. His face looked bloated with flesh around those eyes of his, puffy and dark, although still formidable. I thought perhaps he was hungover. "What are you going to do?" he asked.

"Maybe it would help if you went there and looked for her yourself," I said, baiting the hook.

"To Palm Desert? Today?"

"People will be more forthcoming to a husband and father than a couple of private snoops," I offered.

He nodded. "I'll have to rearrange my schedule. Are you coming down too?"

"No, now that we have a good idea where she is, Roddy is doing some computer work on a variety of the resorts, phone records and so forth. Maybe Candace will leave a computer record for us to find. I'm recanvassing some of the people we've interviewed to see if they can narrow down where your wife and daughter are hiding

out. That's why I'm here." I looked over my shoulder to the receptionist behind him. "And you didn't make that any easier. It looks like you scared the shit out of that woman. Don't make my job harder, Calvin," I said, using his Christian name for the first time, trying to draw him closer to me, to foster false allegiance. "Stay away from people who might be harboring her or harboring information about her."

"You really think I should go to Palm Desert and show Candace and Sherry's photos around? It seems like something you should be doing."

I shook my head. "People will be much more receptive to you. And it won't do any good for you to talk to her friends. She's likely poisoned them against you. They won't tell you anything. I'll handle them. Have you been anywhere else?"

He looked sheepishly at me. "I just came from A Brand New Me."

"Who'd you yell at?"

He smiled at that. "That bossy one. Skinny counselor."

"Sandy Jenkins?"

"Yeah, her. She knew something too. Her face was all sad for a moment. Then angry. I know she wasn't telling me something."

"Let me handle her. How soon can you get to Palm Desert? We do need your help up there."

Grabber met my eyes. "I'll have to go to the office, get my secretary to reschedule my appointments for the next few days. Then I'll go home and pack. I can be there by late evening." He turned and left without another word. He was a man not big on goodbyes.

With Grabber out of the way, I left without talking to the priest or anyone else at the rectory. Then I picked up the donuts and went back to Roddy's to feed the bear some bear claws.

* * * * *

"I've got six possibilities. Tonya Tannin, Elizabeth Vanner, Kim Barnes and three Jane Does."

I brushed powdered sugar off my nose. "Okay, and what have you learned about those six?"

"Weird stuff. And that's what's strange. Tannin and Barnes were both issued new driver's licenses. Tannin, Vanner and Barnes all had cosmetic work done by good Dr. Maglioni. There's no new driver's license issued for Vanner. There were six death certificates issued at the morgue last month on Jane Does—all delivered from the city's indigent hospice. And I know nothing about the three extra stiffs."

"And as regards to the facial recognition program?" I asked.

"Vanner and Barnes are both wearing glasses in their driver's license photos on the DMV website, so the best the computer could do was give me a partial. Neither woman got ruled out, but the Vanner photo on her license is an old one, issued before Candace Grabber disappeared."

"So that would appear to rule Vanner out. How about Tannin?" I inquired.

"She's black, so I'm guessing she's out."

I laughed. "Yeah, I guess Maglioni is not that good at cosmetic surgery."

Roddy motioned at the box of donuts and I handed him another. He scarfed it up in three bites. "Any electronic records on Barnes or the Jane Does? Something to give us a place to start?" I asked.

Roddy shrugged his head no. "Nothing except the two mugshots in the DMV system." He showed me the first photo. A roughly 40-year-old woman with geometric spiky red hair. She wore tortoise-shelled brown glasses. Her face was fair. She did not have buck teeth. She was not attractive. Not someone you would give a second glance on the street. Could it be Candace Grabber? I realized she'd had cosmetic surgery, someone had dyed and cut her hair, bought her new clothes, and taught her how to apply her makeup. I looked at the photo of Candace Grabber on the desk and then at the DMV shot of Kim Barnes on the computer. I didn't think it was her. Maybe I was wrong.

Roddy switched the screen to the second photo. This photo showed a rather large woman, blonde, messy hair, maybe with some gray working its way into the mix. "Who's this?"

Roddy glanced over at the screen. "That's Elizabeth Vanner's photo. Taken three years ago. She gave about two hundred grand

to A Brand New Me two months ago. Like I said, we have records that she got some cosmetic work done and it was billed to A Brand New Me, but I'm guessing it was someone else using her ID. I'm guessing the woman in this photo is dead."

"But no new driver's license issued with a new photo?"

"No, not here or anywhere in the states. Candace could have decided not to get a new license and simply ran off to Mexico, I suppose."

"Then we won't find her."

He agreed.

"And you got nothing on the Jane Does—nothing except we got three more bodies than we got names."

"Yep, thought my searching might clear things up, but it gave us more questions than answers. What's next?" Roddy asked with his mouth full of donut. He washed it down with cold coffee. The pot had long since turned itself off.

"Well, Detective Young seems to know how each woman started her journey. Let's suppose she was right. Candace wanted to stay local. Maybe we can eliminate some of the names by seeing where they went. Let's check the names against plane tickets. Search for Elizabeth Vanner and Kim Barnes for plane flights. Let's see if we can find a plane ticket booked in the last 60 days for either name. We might be able to eliminate one of them that way."

Roddy long ago created backdoors to the airlines' booking lists so it was a fairly short search. We found Kim Barnes booked on a flight to Miami, Florida, connecting on a commuter to Marathon, Florida. It looked like Kim might be planning on starting anew in Key West or somewhere near there. For now, we agreed Barnes was out. And besides, I didn't think the photo was that of Candace Grabber with a new face.

Detective Young said Candace refused to leave town. However, the fact there was no new driver's license was concerning, but we only had the one name left on the list. Elizabeth Vanner was now the target of our search.

"So where do we find Elizabeth Vanner?" Roddy asked, still munching on donuts. He moved to the fridge, opening a bottle of California brewed specialty beer called Lost Abbey. Finishing the

pastry in his hand, Roddy then lifted the last remaining with the other and took a bite. Then more beer. "Good stuff, Maynard."

I laughed, took the bottle from his hand and took a swig. "Damn, that's good," I said. "Got another?" What the hell! It was almost noon—in Denver.

He nodded to the fridge. "So where next?"

I shrugged, opening my own Lost Abbey. "How 'bout we go back to Ms. Sandy Jenkins? Test Elizabeth Vanner's name on her. See if we get a reaction."

"Okay, and if that doesn't work, we tackle Detective Young for a second go." He paused. "You know it's a little weird how tore up Marla Young is over all of this when everyone else has been so hard core."

"You think she's in deeper emotionally than the others in some way?"

Roddy shrugged. "I don't know. Some people can't hold their sin—just like some people can't hold their booze."

"And you think Marla Young is a teetotaler regarding the consumption of sin? Seems unlikely for someone who's made detective. She would have certainly seen a ton of it on the way up on L.A.'s mean streets. She should be able to hold it together by now—no matter how awful the headlines get."

"Can't say for sure. Know we're both good at it."

I laughed and took another drink. "That is not a compliment."

"Didn't say it was."

* * * * *

Sandy Jenkins was in a pink suit when we dropped in on her day. We could see her standing outside her office, watching us walk toward her. It was past lunch, but she was still drinking coffee. She held a cream-colored Starbucks ceramic travel mug with the button lid. Steam curled from its top whenever she raised it to her pink lip-sticked smackers.

"We're back," Roddy announced as we bypassed the receptionist and walked straight back to Ms. Jenkins' office.

"How wonderful for us all," Jenkins said factiously.

"In detective parlance, this is called a 'follow-up,'" said Roddy, taking the lead this time. "We have a couple more questions. Perhaps you could help us."

She smiled ruefully. "I already told you I don't have any information on Candace Grabber for you. I have no idea where she is. And after that awful man, Calvin Grabber, was in here yesterday yelling and making threats there is no way I'd help you two lead him to Candace. That will never happen."

"Yeah," I responded," sorry about that. Our understanding with him is we'll find Candace and the daughter Sherri, make sure they're okay, but we won't tell him where they are. Mr. Grabber is a bit intense."

"He's abusive."

"Probably," I said. "But he deserves to know if his daughter is okay. We said we would do that much. What can you tell us about Elizabeth Vanner? Do you know where she is?"

My jarring segue got a reaction. Ms. Jenkins' body actually jerked a bit and her eyes popped. It was what social scientists call a revelatory micro-expression—almost a macro. The woman regained her composure in a nanosecond, but she knew we knew she'd given herself away. Bingo.

She countered to cover her faux-paux. "Not after the way Grabber behaved in here yesterday. You get nothing from me."

"The husband's not in town. I sent him on a wild goose chase. He's checking hotel registries in Palm Desert for his wife and child. Evidently," I winked, "there was a Candace Grabber sighting up there in the last couple of days."

"I highly doubt that," Sandy Jenkins replied with a tart reply.

Roddy and I both stared at her. Her face bloomed red and she rolled her eyes toward the ceiling. Jenkins sighed with great lament and motioned us into her office. We entered and she closed the door.

"So, by your comment," Roddy asked, soft-pedaling, "you do know where she is?"

Sandy Jenkins said with a whisper, "I can't give up her name or where she is. I vowed I would never, ever, do that—even upon penalty of imprisonment. I am certainly not telling you two. I 'm

sorry. You seem like decent guys, but Candace Grabbers' husband is a beast. I won't tell."

"You know we could blow the whole organization up. Give it to the cops. Give it to the *L.A. Times.*"

She nodded. "I said I thought you were decent guys. You do that, tell the authorities, then good people, including me and Marla, go to jail. And the women we help will be dragged back to their abusive partners. You will be the force that results in some of them being killed."

"We know that and we agree you are on the side of the angels," Roddy said. "But we have to know the two of them are okay. We need to talk to both Candace and Sherri. You don't know us very well, but we don't quit worth a flying fuck. We'll keep at it. You'll eventually tell us, screw up, or we'll be in your lobby area to question you every morning. You think you'll be able to help a lot of women with two detectives setting up shop in your reception area?"

Jenkins sighed again. "Okay, maybe we can meet partway. Are you two willing to go someplace with me? You'd have to wear blindfolds until we got there. Ride in the back of a panel van where you can't see out. You up for that?"

Roddy met my glance. "Sure," we both said at the same time. "Let's do it."

Sandy Jenkins laughed. "You aren't even going to ask where I'm taking you?"

Roddy laughed. "Lady, I figure you ain't going to shoot us in the head and leave our bodies in Sepulveda Basin after dark."

Jenkins laughed. "You think not? You are too trusting." Then she led us out back to a white paneled van.

Roddy and I got in the back and waited until a woman we'd never seen before moved behind the wheel. Sandy Jenkins closed the curtain to the front of the vehicle as the three of us sat on the floorboards. She handed a blindfold to me and indicated I should place it on Roddy's face. I did and then Jenkins applied a second blindfold to me. The blindfolds were strips cut from black t-shirts doubled for thickness. Once on, they completely obliterated our vision.

At first I tried to figure out our destination as we moved from Burbank south, but I lost track of the turns. I know after a while I could hear approaching airport traffic overhead and I knew we were someplace close to LAX, maybe El Segundo or the like. It took about 45 minutes of midday traffic, but eventually we slowed, went up a drive inch-by-inch with a fairly steep incline. A garage door went up. We went in. The van came to a stop. I heard a garage door go down and we were at our destination.

Sandy Jenkins said, "We're at our safe house. Please don't attempt to leave the inside of the house or look outside the windows. We have blackout curtains throughout. There are currently three women here awaiting the beginning of their new lives. They will be afraid of you. They are afraid of men. Please do not speak to them. If you have questions, ask me and I'll address them. Are you both okay with these terms?"

"Is Candace Grabber here?"

"No," answered Sandy Jenkins. "She spent several weeks here, but she has been gone for at least a month now. None of the women here ever met her."

We nodded. Our eyes were still adjusting to the light of the garage. We exited the van and followed Sandy Jenkins into the house. It was a large split level. It was furnished, but the furniture was awful—obviously rescued from the dump or off the curb. Everything inside the home was mismatched castoffs. This residence was not finished for comfort. It was a passing through station. The women who stayed were not being encouraged to stay. It was a train station in an underground railroad.

Sandy with some calls up the stairs gathered the three women to the living room and we stood before them. They cowered with trepidation before us—the first men they'd encountered since they disappeared. All were around 40 years of age. One wore two black eyes. Another had her nose packed with cotton. The third wore horn-rimmed glasses and did not meet our gaze.

Roddy tilted his head to me. His fingers raised three fingers for only me to see.

"Have all three of these women here been abused?" I asked Sandy.

Jenkins answered affirmatively, but her role of intermediary was unnecessary. The women answered for themselves, anxious to tell us what horrid men they were with until the last few weeks. They took turns telling their stories. Roddy and I did not speak and simply let them get their words on record. Testifying against their abusive partners.

"Why are your eyes blackened?" Roddy asked. "Did your man hit you?"

"No," said the blonde, "I had some work done. Changin' things up before I start over. New hair color too. They say blondes have more fun. I figure to. I haven't had much fun up to now." Her voice revealed a southern drawl that California living had not been able to strip away.

The third woman in the glasses asked us, "Why are you here? Are you police?"

"No," I said, "we're just looking for one of the women who used to stay here?"

Sandy Jenkins smiled patiently. "Do you ladies think anyone who has come through this safe house wants to be found? Do any of you want to tell these men your old names? Where you came from?"

They laughed at us for the absolutely ridiculous thought that any of them would want to return to the hell which had been their lives before A Brand New Me rescued them.

Soon our interview was over. The women left the room, returning to their bedrooms and out of our sight. "So?" said Sandy Jenkins, "do you see why I can't give you any information on any of these women? I can't and won't divulge any information. I won't let these women down."

"Regardless if we blow your organization up?"

Sandy Jenkins stared at Roddy without speaking after he asked the question. "I saw your face just now. I am banking on the humanity in you not to do that. I believe I'm a good judge of character. You two aren't going to turn us in." She knew from our silence she was right.

Then she took us back, blindfolded in a van, to our vehicle. And that was that.

On the way back to Roddy's place, I glanced over at him as we traveled from Burbank to Malibu. "What can we do when we can't leverage the behavior of A Brand New Me's people because they know our threats are empty ones? That we won't actually go to the cops? I'm guessing you are in agreement, we aren't going to turn them in.

"Hell no," Roddy answered. "I feel like we ought to write 'em a check, not turn 'em in."

"Agreed. So, what's next?" I asked my partner.

"Let me do some computer work once everyone goes to bed tonight. Karen and Gracie will be home about the time we get there. Maybe I can find something."

* * * * *

I drove home to the trailer in Topanga for the night. I prepared good steaks on the grill for both my semi-pet coyote Dapper and me. The coyote drifted down into the clearing by the trailer at dusk after I arrived home and started the grill. I filled his water bowl with a tray of ice cubes and he occasionally took a sip while he waited for his steak. Dapper seemed to know my head was full of conflicted thoughts so he tried to cheer me up. He went down to the concrete pool and rolled onto his back, waiting for me to come and give him a quick scrub with some Dawn dishwater soap I kept in a bottle there. Dapper allowed me to scratch his belly, rinse him and put on a new flea collar. Then after shaking water over me, he trotted to the trailer and lay on the cool metal steps. I joined him and sat on the first step, finishing a beer and watching the sun fall over the hills of Topanga. When I moved inside for the evening, he followed me in and lay on the cool laminated floor as the air conditioner hummed on high. I put on Ronnie Woods' "Gimmee Some Neck" and cleaned my guns with an oily rag until I was tired enough to sleep. Dapper curled in a ball at the foot of my bed, his nose aimed at the door, ever vigilant, ready to bolt through the opening I had installed for his use.

I slept fitfully, dreaming of a safe house filled with women with black eyes, packed noses and fear in their hearts. I did not rest well and was awake when the phone rang at not quite 5:00 am. Dapper jolted to movement with the first ring and was out the dog door

into the night. I knew I would not see him again until the sun fell once again. He was gone, back to the pack that gathered in the hills high up above Mullholland. It was good Dapper still ran with his pack when I was away. I was away a lot. I picked up the phone, expecting it to be Roddy. It was.

"What you got?" I asked.

"A body."

"What?"

"A body," Roddy repeated. "Elizabeth Vanner was cremated in Tulsa, Oklahoma, her hometown, three weeks ago."

"What the fuck? But the real Elizabeth Vanner was buried in a potter's field by L.A. County, right?"

"Yeah, well, someone else got burned to a crisp in Tulsa. Probably Candace. Get down here." He hung up.

I hightailed it down to Malibu in record time, beating morning rush hour traffic to the punch for once.

* * * * *

It was already normal business hours in Tulsa, Oklahoma, which was on central time, when I arrived at Roddy's. We were able to talk by phone to the funeral home director who answered on the first ring. He himself worked on Elizabeth Vanner's body when it arrived by air transport to the funeral home from Los Angeles. He told us the deceased was shipped from the Los Angeles city morgue, funds paid by an anonymous donor according to the notes in his Vanner file, which he forwarded to us by email as we spoke.

"I see," I said into the speaker phone over my cup of coffee as Roddy printed the documents in the folder. "Does the manifest for the body give a cause of death?"

"Oh yes," said the mortician in somewhat a patronizing tone, "all shipping of a deceased person requires a standard death certificate which includes cause of death."

"And can you go to the record and tell us what it was? I don't see that document at first glance."

"Oh, I don't need to do that. I remember quite well. It was a fractured skull caused by blunt force trauma. Car accident. I remember it quite well because of the damage to Ms. Vanner's

face. It was quite unusual. Horrible damage, although she must have been quite loved by someone."

"Why do you say that?"

"Well, as I said she died of blunt force trauma, but she'd had substantial cosmetic work done just before her death. There had been no healing whatsoever. Good work too, expensive. But then, in contrast, her nose was a mess, broken and smashed beyond any repair. I was relieved the instructions were for cremation. We would not have been able to have an open casket service. I guess it didn't matter too much since she only had a single person at the service. Not one family member. And I don't think the one mourner even signed the register. Sad thing, isn't it? To die so alone without a single friend or family member in attendance."

"The person who attended the service was not a little girl about ten?"

"Oh no," replied the mortician. "It was a cop. The lady cop from L.A who accompanied Ms. Vanner's remains upon their final journey. She seemed to care very much about Ms. Vanner. Cried quite a lot. I must say I was impressed. You know, Los Angeles police have had such bad press in the last few years."

* * * * *

"Spill it," Roddy growled at the female detective coming off duty. She'd almost made it to her car after her shift. We stood by the vehicle, flanking the female detective.

Detective Marla Young looked at Roddy with surprise. It was not yet eight a.m. At first, her eyes just registered the amazement that we were there, but then the fatigue of the night shift rapidly reentered her eyes. Then they moved to sadness and resignation. Marla Young nodded, stopping a few feet before she reached us, but then said, "Not here." She glanced around to see if anyone noticed us, but we were alone. "Somewhere I can get a drink."

We found a 24-hour Irish joint far enough from the station that no cops frequented it. Detective Young slid into a booth. The bartender seemed to know her from other mornings after other night shifts. She ordered a Jim Bean double.

"What do you know?" she asked in a deadpan voice as her bourbon and our two coffees arrived.

"That you attended Elizabeth Vanner's funeral in Tulsa, Oklahoma three weeks ago. Except it wasn't Elizabeth Vanner because Elizabeth Vanner died at the city's indigent hospice about a month before that. It was Candace Grabber cremated in Tulsa. She died of blunt force trauma. Beaten to death, but the death certificate falsely reported it as a car wreck. That's what we think. We'll be able to prove it eventually if we have to. So, is it true?" Roddy's eyes sparked fire as he accused her.

Detective Marla Young began to cry. She wept aloud and the bartender started to walk over, but Roddy waved a hand menacingly his way and the barkeep veered away from the table in response.

"Yes," She paused. "It's true." Her voice caught as she spoke. Then she bawled audibly. We were the only customers in the joint and there was no pity at our table. The barkeep kept his eyes off of us.

"And it was her husband? He found her at the safe house and killed her and you let him get away with it. To save your underground railroad operation—to save all your asses, you let him get away with murder."

Detective Young sat forward. Her face registered complete shock and confusion. "No," she said in a whisper. "You got it all wrong. She died on the operating table at Maglioni's on Rodeo Drive. The volunteer doctor over at A Brand New Me gave her a cursory physical, signed her health certificate and cleared her for cosmetic surgery prior to her appointment. The day she died, Maglioni started his surgery on her eyes, getting rid of her sagging eyelids. Next he was going to give her a nose job and fix that overbite of hers, but the clinic doctor missed a hairline fracture at her temple. I figure it was from the last beating that son-of-a-bitch of a husband gave her. When Maglioni used the mallet to break her nose, the impact caused the fracture to split on her skull and she died within a minute. Nothing he could do."

It took a minute or so for that to sink in. I was silent, but my partner was not. Roddy snorted in disgust. "Let me guess the next part. You waited until dark and then smuggled the body out like so much medical waste. You took her to the morgue where you already had a co-conspirator lined up and made out a faked death

certificate. Then you shipped the body off to her 'quote/unquote' hometown where you knew nobody was left to give a good goddamn."

"Yes," she gasped and waved to the bar man for another drink. This time Roddy let him approach the table.

The bartender set the drink down. "Everything okay over here?"

I glared at him. "So fucking not okay you cannot imagine. Now beat it."

He retreated.

Roddy stared back at Detective Young until she couldn't hold his gaze. She dropped her eyes to the double in front of her. She took a slug and kept her eyes at the floor.

"You let two doctors walk on malpractice resulting in death charges to cover your sorry drunken ass?"

Detective Young just nodded. Perhaps thirty seconds passed. Then she said, "Maglioni demanded we indemnify him against any legal action that might be forthcoming or he was going to go to the cops."

"How did you manage that?" I asked.

"We got him paperwork on LAPD stationary that said Elizabeth Vanner was a protected witness in the WITSEC program and he could not go to the police as it would tip off those whom she was testifying against. He could not report she was dead because it would jeopardize the FBI's attempt to push a plea deal. He would be responsible for putting killers back on the street. Maglioni knew it was bullshit, but he took the letter and filed it with his attorney for protection should he need it."

"Guy's no dummy. He's kept himself pretty insulated all the way through this shit storm," I said.

Detective Young nodded.

"One last question about Candace Grabber," Roddy stated, "before we move on to talk about the daughter."

"Okay," Detective Young was not trying to hide anything now. "What?"

"Maglioni's mallet didn't mess up Elizabeth Vannick's nose so badly that they would have had to have a closed casket service. What the hell happened?"

Detective Young looked at us with tears in her eyes, but it was a new look—one of shame. She didn't want to reveal this last horror. Roddy let her stay silent for a second, but then he gripped her arm and began to squeeze, just a little. "Let it all out. You're gonna have to tell it all now—or..." He didn't finish.

"I tried to hide the cosmetic work before we took the body to the morgue. I thought there might be questions..." Her tone was pleading, wanting us to understand.

"You tried to hide it how?" Roddy voice was guttural and fierce.

The air was rarified at our table. Detective Young looked as grim and devastated as anyone I've ever seen. She stared at Roddy as she answered his question. "I hit her with a phone book. It took a few times." And then Detective Young began to cry, her muffled words descending to a depth like a ship sinking into a very dark and desolate sea.

* * * * *

It took a while for Marla Young to regain a semblance of composure, but we eventually got an address for where Sherri Grabber was being sheltered by the nuns at a convent in Munro Bay, a small village on the ocean just north of San Luis Obispo. We headed there immediately. Looking back as we left the bar, I did not think Detective Young would attempt to thwart us. I did worry she would commit suicide, so as we sped northward I called Speedy Khuzaymah, a close friend and a detective for the force. I told him Detective Marla Young was in the middle of an alcoholic depression and I feared she might harm herself. I gave him the address. He promised to handle it personally. I knew he would—with discretion and sensitivity.

* * * * *

We reached the convent by noon and it was a wonder we didn't get a speeding ticket on the way up. Roddy hauled ass all the way up the PCH.

When we arrived at the convent, a large granite block building with a Spanish style, red ceramic tiled roof, I stood, stretching my leg. My stump ached. The convent was really a castle, or at least a

tower and ramparts of white-washed adobe, thick and old. We climbed the many steps to the front door, knocked and asked to speak to whomever was in charge. The Mother Superior, we were told politely by the shy, freckly nun who answered the door, would see us in the convent's library. The novice led us to a large room filled with old religious texts. There set a desk and two chairs opposite it in the shadows of the bookshelves.

A nun of about 70 years of age entered. She was stooped with arthritis and had to turn her head to her side to greet us out beyond the white bandeau scarf which held her gray-streaked coif to her head. The woman waved us to sit and we did. It took a few moments, but she rounded the desk and sank slowly with some evident pain into the leather chair. The old woman leaned far back so she might meet our eyes without having to arch her bent neck.

"Welcome to our home. I am Sister Alyssa. And you are?"

We told her. Then she asked what she could do for us. We told her that too.

She released to us a muted smile without any humor in it, but still with a dollop of good will. "Yes, I always knew someday someone from the rough-and-tumble world we live in would show up and ask about Sherri."

Roddy leaned forward. " Sherri Grabber is here?"

"She is called Sherri Vanner now, but yes, she is here."

"And she is okay?"

Sister Alyssa frowned. "No, I would not say she is okay. She has been through a lot. Her family broke apart. Her father is a violent man who hurt her mother. His violence ultimately led to her death, although indirectly. This young woman has lost all of her world. Everything. Well, except her faith. It is a blessing this young lady has unusually strong faith. It has taken all the faith in her heart to get her through this situation. She is still very fragile."

I nodded solemnly. "She knows her mother is dead?"

"Yes, but not the circumstances, per se. She knows her mother went into the hospital and died. She does not know, nor needs to know, the details. She will be told in due time. Years from now. Perhaps it will be me who will tell her. God willing, it will be. If not, the next to oversee the convent will do so."

Roddy looked a bit sheepish. "And the money? Candace Grabber had a half million in cash when she left her husband."

Sister Alyssa frowned. "And is that why you are here? For the money? I am disappointed."

Roddy frowned right back. "No, you misunderstand. Our mission is to make sure the girl is okay. That she is taken care of. That her future is secure. We don't want any of Candace's cash."

"But you are detectives for hire. Someone is paying you to find her. Is it the father?" Mother Alyssa shook her head disapprovingly. She stood and moved around until her bent neck put her face over ours, forcing us to peer upward at her. She pointed a finger, lamenting our client.

"And now you have found her. Should I expect that violent man, the man who destroyed this little girl's life, killed her mother, to show up on my doorstep since you have found us? Are you a harbinger of an evil wind?"

"No, the father will never know she is here. That is, if we are convinced she is safe and will be cared for. That you have not offered her sanctuary in order to get the money."

Sister Alyssa raised her eyebrows. "You are rather forthright. Are you accusing us of greed? You know we have taken a vow of poverty."

Roddy grinned. "I guess I just did, yeah. Just being straight up. Can't lie to a nun, right?" He shrugged, not caring. "What's the deal with the moola, Sister?"

She smiled broadly, liking Roddy like everyone always did. "The moola, as you call it, is safe. Before the surgery, Candace— well, Elizabeth Vanner put the entire remaining 450,000 dollars into a trust. The fund in which it is invested pays a five percent return. The convent will receive the roughly $20,000 dividend each year to raise the girl. She will live here and attend a local parochial school. When Sherri is ready for college, the head of the convent, with power of attorney, will help Sherri determine her educational needs and her college education will be paid out of the trust. Any remaining funds will be available to her once she graduates college or at age 26, whichever comes first. I will give you the name of the trust manager so you may verify this information is true. I trust you will keep it confidential?"

"Of course," Roddy said crisply with a tiny salute.

"Would you like to see her? If you do not mind, I will allow you to see her from a distance, but I would rather you did not speak to her. She is still confused and unsure of herself and her future. She keeps asking if she is going to be forced to leave here. I hope you understand."

Roddy nodded. He was now a fan of Sister Alyssa. The two decided they like the cut of the other's jib—whatever a jib was. I was simply along for the ride.

Sister Alyssa led us up a round spiral of adobe stairs. We made it to the tower and we looked over the beach area below, but it was not one of sun and sand. It was gravel strewn and the angry waves attacked the eroded shoreline. It was a beach for someone who'd been battered. From our vantage, we could clearly see the girl. Three of the younger nuns, probably all in their 20's, were with her and the four kicked a soccer ball around between them. We could see even from our distance that Sherri Vannick was all smiles. She was smaller than the others, but was speedy and lithe. Once she got the ball away from the nuns and dribbled it into a natural alcove from the waves. She kicked the ball into a mound of boulders, her imaginary net, yelling "Goal," garnering laughs from her playmates and keepers. She danced with her arms spread in the air.

Sherri's face turned upward and she recognized Sister Alyssa in the distance at the building's zenith. The girl also saw the two men beside her. Her face, I could tell, clouded with concern for a moment, but Sister Alyssa smiled broadly and waved in an exaggerated way, letting the ten-year-old know all was fine in her world. I smiled too, realizing it was time to leave.

* * * * *

Late that afternoon, we returned downtown to the office. Roddy dropped me on the street while he drove his truck around to the garage. I bought us two coffees in the lobby. With two dark roasts in hand, I rode the elevator up, exited, set the coffees on the floor and used my key to enter the office. I went back and retrieved the beverages, bending over to get them off the floor. The elevator door rang. I heard the door open, but didn't look up. I assumed it

was Roddy entering. "Java Jones at your service," I quipped. But it was Calvin Grabber. And he was in a fury.

"You sent me up there to get me out of the way. Decoyed me and wasted my time. I finally figured it out." He pushed me back into the office, the coffees splashing onto the carpet as I dropped them. He chest-bumped me, and his thick thighs banging into my false leg and it buckled. I only stumbled for an instant, Calvin Grabber misinterpreted my sudden move. He grappled at the front of my shirt with both hands, and I stomped with my good foot on his instep. He howled with pain and toppled back into the desk. Grabber removed one hand from my shirt and grabbed the far edge of the desk for leverage. I used the advantage to force him back and further off balance.

Grabber drew back to punch me, one hand still on the desk for leverage, but suddenly Roddy was coming through the door. My partner waded into trouble as I knew he was born to do. With his big right paw, he grabbed the thick wrist of Grabber's which was still drawing back. Roddy, with his right hand like a vice on Grabber's wrist, forced the man to tuck at the waist. Grabber's face went down onto the desk by his left hand. Roddy opened the drawer and six inches and then slammed it hard. Hard as hell. Fingers lipped over the edge broke like kindling and Grabber screamed like something inhuman. The injured man yanked his hand free, but Roddy slammed two open palms into the Grabber's shoulders. The man, pain still registering in his face, fell backwards onto the floor in front of us. He was momentarily surprised, not used to being outmuscled, but Roddy did not hesitate. He whipped his weapon from his right shoulder holster. It was a huge silver plated British Webley with a seven-inch barrel. The gun sight on the barrel was nearly three-quarters of an inch high. Roddy slapped Grabber's face with the long barrel, grinding it and its sight into Grabber's face, cutting a long mean furrow that showed red along the man's left cheek. Grabber crumpled onto the floor.

"You broke all my fingers," Grabber whined, his good hand holding his damaged one like a drowned kitten.

"Jerk off with the other hand, you sick son-of-a-bitch. Your fingers are the least of your worries. I'm about to blow your

fucking head off." Roddy was shaking with anger. The skin around his temples was purple and pulsing.

Grabber's eyes increased in size by approximately three times. "Why? What for? For grabbing your friend? I didn't even hit him. I was just trying to scare him enough so he would tell me where my wife and daughter are."

Roddy laughed and looked at me. "Grace here doesn't scare worth a damn. I've seen him run right at a whole building full of wild-eyed Baathists shooting AKs at him. You," he slapped the gun barrel against Grabber's ear, drawing blood. "You," he repeated. "You don't scare either of us. But that doesn't mean I'm not going to blow your fucking brains all over that wall behind you."

"Why? Why?"

"Because you beat her. You beat your wife bad. Candace ran from you and then you hired us to do your dirty work and find her. Your end game was for us to bring her home so you could beat her again. Or maybe you didn't want her back. Maybe you just wanted that half a million of hers. And we took your money to find her. I'm ashamed." He slapped the gun barrel against Grabber's ear again. "And I don't like being ashamed of my behavior. I have a woman and a daughter in my life now and I'm trying to be a better man."

Grabber began to blubber. Roddy rapped him really hard with the gun against the crown of his skull this time. Blood dripped down from his hairline onto his white collar, creating a stark red stain.

Roddy put the barrel between Grabber's eyes and cocked the gun. It grew intensely quiet in the room. Grabber wet himself. "What can I do?"

Roddy laughed. "You mean besides get some adult diapers? Well, first you promise you're going to stop looking for your wife. We've verified Candace is someplace you'll never come close to finding. You will never come close to her. You try and find her, I kill you. You come after us, we got a band of brothers who will kill you. I will leave instructions and a sniper rifle to my whole mentally unstable army unit to take you off the board if anything happens to either Grace here or me. Got it?"

"Okay, okay. I don't even want Candace back, but my daughter. I need... I want..." he sobbed. "I want Sherri back. I love her."

I wanted to shout, "But you killed her mother, the person she loved most in life," but I did not. Roddy was currently perfect in his role of deranged bad cop. I remained silent.

Roddy paused, selecting his next words carefully. "I've looked over your accounting. I've seen your bank records. I know you have about three million liquid floating about in various banks. I also know you didn't pay taxes on some of it."

Grabber sneered, "So you're going to blackmail me by threatening an IRS action. That hardly would be as bad as the assault charges I could file on you."

Roddy dipped his chin toward me. "I got someone to testify you were assaulting him when I came into the office. Doesn't even need to be true, although it is. We'd probably embellish. No, I don't give a shit about your little tax loophole hideaways. I care about your daughter's future."

Grabber narrowed his eyes at Roddy. He still held his damaged hand gingerly. It trembled as he clinched it to his chest. "I care about my daughter much more than you."

"Your behavior to the contrary," Roddy smirked. "I'm going to let you prove it to me. You're going to leave here, go to the emergency room and get your hand fixed. You're going to tell the doctors that you closed your fingers in your car door. Make sure you stick to that story because I will check."

"Okay, and then what?" Grabber's eyes had regained a little balance. He was still crying, but now it might have been shame, but the shame was in being bested by Roddy, not what he had done to his wife. It made me sick.

"Then you're going to take some information I'm going to give you. There's a bank official in downtown Santa Barbara. You're going to tell that bank official to put a cool million tomorrow into a blind trust to go to your daughter upon her 26th birthday. I will make sure Candace knows you've done so with the best of intentions. You are bidding them farewell and wishing them well. You are giving a million bucks to your little girl to make sure she

is well cared for. Her mother's money will certainly be enough to get them through until Sherri is an adult."

Grabber shook his head no. "I need to see her. She's my little girl."

Roddy took the Webley sighted barrel and rammed it roughly into Grabber's nose. It began to bleed down his face and into his mouth. He began to sob again. "Okay, okay, I'll do it." His words were indistinct with the blood in his mouth and gun barrel stuck in his nostril.

"Any variation, you end up with a pie plate sized hole out the back of your head. We got a deal?"

"Yes." Grabber dropped his gaze to the floor, a defeated and crushed man.

Roddy drew the barrel back out of Grabber's nose, carving yet another channel. "Then get out of here. And you should know, I bugged every one of your electronic devices when I was at your house. You so much as think of calling the cops or anyone else and we'll know, so don't even try. And even if you would get us— though you're not man enough—but if you did, it wouldn't matter. You would be dead before dark the day you did us in. We have very violent friends."

Grabber staggered to his feet. He grabbed the door handle with his good hand.

"Grabber?" Roddy called to the man with blood mixing with tears across his smeared face. "You have until the end of business tomorrow to deposit the money into the trust. Before 5:00 pm. If you don't do it, I'm hunting you by dark."

Grabber nodded and stumbled out the door.

When the door closed, Roddy switched off his act. He turned to me and smiled with a sorrowful look. "Almost five o'clock here, buddy. We got nothing to do for 24 hours. What do you say we drive up to Monro Bay in the morning and donate the ten grand Grabber paid us to the convent? Can't really keep it, right?"

I was stunned at Roddy's change in mood—the rage turning to pleasantry in but a second—but decided to go with it. "Sure, there's a really good barbeque place in Santa Barbara. Wanna keep enough cash out to buy side of ribs for both of us? Really tie one on after we take the check to Sister Alyssa?"

"Nah, let's give her the whole enchilada. Ribs are on me." Roddy beamed at me as he put his gun back in the holster.

"You know we're letting Grabber walk on a murder, although he doesn't even know his wife is dead, but he killed her," I said.

"Yeah," Roddy answered, "but if we filed on him, then the whole Brand New Me gang goes to prison. They are saving lives. I can't do. How 'bout you?"

"Nope," I replied, "me neither. Hey Rod, that Webley didn't even have a round in the chamber when you cocked it, did it?" I laughed.

"Nah," he acknowledged. "I only carry it for that bad ass sight on the barrel. Sharpen that baby with a flint stone every night."

"Ouch," I said. "You know, when you stuck it in his nose all I could think of was the scene when Roman Polanski cuts Jack Nicholson's nose in *Chinatown*."

"Me too, man. Me too." We both laughed.

"What you gonna do tonight, Roddy?"

"I got two ladies training me to be a better man tonight. How about you?"

"Coyote and me having burgers off the grill. Wanna trade?"

"Not a chance, Gracer. Not a chance in the world."

Made in the USA
Lexington, KY
04 September 2017